25 days

25 days

PER JACOBSEN

HUMBLEBOOKS

25 DAYS

Dear Reader,

This book is my version of an advent calendar, meaning that each day in December, up until the 25th, brings a new chapter—and the events in each chapter unfold on the same date within the story.

Ideally, you would read one chapter each day as you count down to Christmas. In the end, though, the choice is entirely yours, and you are free to read it however you like.

Merry Christmas!

—Per Jacobsen

"You better watch out.
You better not cry."

—HAVEN GILLESPIE

December 1st

Adam

It's pure reflex. As soon as the first few notes of Mariah Carey's *All I Want for Christmas* have found their way to his ears, Adam Gray's hand releases its grip on the steering wheel and moves down to the radio's volume knob.

He doesn't turn it, though. Something makes him hesitate and change his mind. Perhaps it's the realization that he's the only one of the four people in the vehicle who has registered the music.

In the past, the two girls in the back seat would have ordered him to crank up the volume—and the woman in the passenger seat would have belted along from the very first line, not worrying about key or rhythm. Now, they just sit there, staring at glass plates; the girls on the screens of their cell phones and Beth on the pane of the side window.

In the past. It's a strong phrase to use for something

that doesn't go further back than a few years. It's crazy how so much can change in such a short time.

Outside the car, the air is full of dancing snow-flakes, and the pines whizzing by on both sides have been given a touch of white on top of their evergreen needles.

So has the asphalt of the road, which Adam isn't too happy about. Especially not if it gets worse. True, they can also get large amounts of snow in Newcrest, where they live, but it usually doesn't take very long before the first snowplows are sent out to clear the roads.

But they are up north now. Far from Newcrest, and far from major cities in general. And Adam has a strong feeling that these deserted roads that wind through the Willowbend forests aren't exactly at the top of the clearing crew's itinerary.

But that was kind of the point, wasn't it? he thinks. *To get away from it all and spend some quality time together as a family.*

He glances over at Beth in the passenger seat. She sits with one leg pulled up so that her foot is resting on the seat and her chin on her knee. He can't see her face because it's still turned toward the window, and her freckled cheek is hidden away behind a thick lock of chestnut-brown hair.

She has been gazing at the landscape almost non-stop throughout the drive. Three hours of her just staring blankly out the window ... although Adam has a feeling that she isn't so much looking at the landscape as she is avoiding looking at him.

He moves his gaze up to the rearview mirror just in time to see his eldest daughter move her hand up in front of her mouth as if she is suppressing a burst of laughter.

"What's so funny?" he asks.

Abby jolts when she realizes that she is the one he is talking to, and she slams the phone down on her thigh with the speed of a furious cobra.

"Nothing," she says. "Just something on TikTok."

Adam opens his mouth, then sees the expression in her eyes in the rearview mirror and thinks twice. No need to start a war by asking her for more details.

While her older sister picks up her phone again, Chloe momentarily takes her eyes off her trance-inducing screen and leans in between the front seats.

"How much further is it?"

"In about half an hour we'll be at the gas station where we're supposed to meet the guy who owns the cabin," Adam replies. "He's going to take us the rest of the way up there. How far that is, I don't know, but it's probably not that bad."

"Why don't we just meet at the cabin?"

Adam turns around in his seat and glances at her with one eyebrow raised.

"Because it's a vacation in the *country* that I've booked for us," he says. "And when you're out in the country, like *really* out in the country, the GPS gets confused."

He emphasizes the last word by crossing his eyes and tilting his head from side to side before moving his gaze back to the windshield. This makes nine-year-old Chloe let out a giggle—and her fifteen-year-old sister roll her eyes.

One in three he can still get a smile from. Guess that's better than nothing. In any case, it's what he will have to settle for. However, he is hoping that this vacation might change that a bit.

In the speakers, Mariah Carey's only Christmas wish fades out, and a news fanfare takes over. After that follows a deep male voice.

"Straight from WBCN's studio in Colmena, this is Mark Ranter, wishing you a good afternoon and welcoming you to the news on this bitterly cold first of December. We start off in Grismond, where a family with children woke up this morning to an unpleasant —and rather macabre—start to the Christmas month. It was the father who made the chilling discovery on his way out with the garbage. He spotted a bloody trail leading into the family's garage. And what he found in there was nothing short of a horrendous sight. Someone had hanged—"

A click, and the voice is gone. Adam looks down and sees Beth's fingers clutching the dial on the radio. From it, his gaze slides up and meets hers.

She looks angry. Judgmental.

"What?" he says, gesturing down to the radio. "I'm not the one who decides what they say on the news, am I?"

"No, but you are able to decide what your daughters need to listen to, aren't you?"

He doesn't know what bothers him the most. What she's saying, or the way she says it. The way she whispers it, as if that would somehow prevent the two girls in the back seat from hearing it. Christ, they're sitting less than four feet away from her. And on top of that, she has just turned off the radio.

Adam's teeth dig into the flesh on the inside of his lip, but he manages to maintain a smile on the outside. Which is good, because he has promised himself that he won't argue with Beth on this trip. He wants to course-correct the ship, not sink it.

"I ... I didn't really listen to it," he says. "My head was in a completely different place. But you're right. Sorry."

He looks at her, she stares at him, and then—*luckily* —she nods and leans back in her seat. Catastrophe avoided.

Half an hour of awkward silence later, Adam turns the car into the parking lot in front of the Exxon gas station, a short distance outside the town of Crimson.

The town. Using that word to describe Crimson is almost a stretch. How many houses did they pass between the WELCOME TO CRIMSON sign and the NOW LEAVING CRIMSON sign? Ten? Fifteen?

"What a fucking ghost town," Abby mumbles in the back seat.

"Hey, language!" both parents yell in chorus ... but after a short pause, Beth leans toward Adam and whispers:

"Who the hell taught those little fuckers to talk like that?"

Adam feels his lips pulling up in a smile. Partly because that sentence is an old inside joke between him and Beth, but even more so because she also smiles at him. That happens so rarely these days. Maybe this trip really is what's needed to get them back on track.

"You're not wrong, though, Abby. It didn't exactly look overpopulated," he replies as he lets his gaze wander first across the roof above the gasoline pumps and then down to the facade of the gas station's store. Both look like something from a different era. Rust and cracked paint mar the bottom side of the snow-covered roof, and the windows of the store look like they haven't been cleaned since Clinton resided in the White House.

"Looks like we got here first," Adam says, turning to the girls in the back seat. "How about we take a quick look in the store to see if they've got some candy?"

The response is as surprising as it is heartbreaking. Both girls wrinkle their noses and shrug, not even bothering to lift their gazes from their phones.

"What the heck is wrong with their generation?" he

mumbles to Beth. "I would have pushed my little brother down a well for a bag of Skittles at their age."

She smiles again—and it feels as though his lungs finally get a bit of oxygen after an eternity without.

"Well, if you are going in there anyway," Abby says, "I wouldn't mind a Coke."

"Oh yeah, me too!" Chloe adds.

He glances at Beth, who responds by shaking her head slightly.

"Your word is my command, your highnesses," he jokes, making a theatrical bow to the girls as he gets out of the car. "You just stay seated and leave the Coke quest to me. We wouldn't want you straining your legs after such a long drive, now, would we?"

Snow crunches beneath his feet, and the air is still full of swirling flakes as Adam walks over to the store. Once in a while, some of them land in the stubble of his cheeks and are transformed into chilly water droplets that run down his neck, making him shudder.

When the motion sensor on the wall above the store entrance detects his presence, the glass doors slide apart, revealing a room that looks exactly as Adam imagined it would.

It's dim, due to a burnt-out fluorescent tube in the ceiling, which no one has bothered to replace, and practically every shelf has a thin coating of light gray dust.

The floor tiles are also pretty dirty. A few of them have broken loose in the joints, making them creak underneath Adam's shoes as he moves through the room.

The counter is at the opposite end of the store. Behind it is a clerk chatting with the only other customer; a brawny man in coveralls, holding a rolled-up newspaper in a fist that looks as if it could pulverize a pool ball without any problems.

Adam edges past a rotating rack filled with various snacks and sweets in colorful packaging and walks over to a fridge on the left side of the store. It's not very big, and two of the shelves are almost completely empty, but he still finds what he needs; a bottle of water and two cans of Coke.

Carrying these, he continues over to the counter, where the clerk has turned his back and is putting up a poster on the back wall—a drowsy man behind the wheel of a car and a reminder that the store sells freshly brewed coffee every day for only two bucks.

In the meantime, the big man in the coveralls has started reading his newspaper. Nevertheless, he is still standing right in front of the counter—and he stays there, even as Adam queues up behind him and clears his throat.

"Excuse me, sir. Are you standing in line?"

The man lifts his head and glances at him. Then he —slowly—runs his tongue over his front teeth, causing his upper lip to bulge.

"Do I look like I'm standing in line?"

For a moment, Adam is completely paralyzed by

that answer, and he can't find any words, let alone utter them. The fact that the man appears even bigger up close doesn't exactly help either.

"I ... um, no. It was just ... well, you were reading your paper, and ..."

"And I'm not allowed to do that, or what? Or maybe you don't think a hillbilly like me *can* read at all? That it?"

"I ... what? No, I just figured that you probably weren't standing in line because you were reading."

"Come on, Sam," the clerk drones behind the counter. He is an older guy, and the tone of his voice reveals that this isn't the first time he has had to reprimand his regular customer. "The poor guy thinks you're being serious. And it's not like I'm flooded with customers as it is. If you keep scaring them away, I won't have any at all."

The big man in the coveralls squints at the clerk and rolls his eyes. Then he turns his gaze back to Adam's face, studying it carefully, while his tongue takes another trip across his front teeth. Then his lips spread, exposing a tobacco-stained set of teeth.

"We like to mess a bit with strangers that wander out here into the middle of nowhere," he says, as if that one sentence explains and justifies everything. "Especially if they're city slickers."

I see. What a great joke. Netflix hasn't called to offer you a stand-up special yet?

Even though that's what he thinks, Adam just nods

and pulls up his lips in the tiniest smile he can get away with.

The man in the coveralls takes a step back, and Adam edges his way past. As he passes him, he inhales a mixture of sweat and motor oil that gives him a sting of nausea. Luckily, the man doesn't stay behind him for very long before he closes the newspaper and strolls toward the exit.

"Anything else?" the elderly gentleman behind the counter asks.

Adam shakes his head.

"No thanks, just this."

The clerk nods and taps a bony finger on top of the cash register's display where the amount is shown in digital numbers.

"Three bucks and twenty," he says—and while Adam looks for the change in his wallet, he leans over the counter and whispers: "Don't mind Sam. He's all bark and no bite."

"It's okay," Adam says with a strained, polite smile on his lips.

"Always was a bit of a weirdo," the clerk continues. "Shouldn't come as a surprise, though. Lived with his mom all his life. *All* his life. Can you imagine?"

"It's okay," Adam repeats because he has no idea what else to say. "Nothing happened."

The clerk nods as he reaches out his hand to take the payment. Sadly, Adam doesn't have the exact change ... because at this point, he really just wants to get away from this chatty old geezer.

But no, he has to wait nicely while the elderly gentleman behind the counter finds his change. And there is no rush.

"I see you have your family sitting out in the car. Are you passing through?"

"Yes and no. We're supposed to meet with someone out here. We've rented a vacation house."

The clerk squints his eyes and nods in a strangely knowing way. Then he raises his index finger and points it at Adam.

"It's Bill's cabin, isn't it?"

Adam responds with silence and a fairly reluctant nod, hoping that might help to end the conversation.

"If you think you're out in the country now, you just wait," the clerk says as he drops the change into Adam's palm. "This is nothing compared to Bill's cabin. It's all the way up where ... oh look, there he is now."

He points out the window, and Adam follows the direction of his finger.

Sure enough, out in the parking lot, a new vehicle has just arrived. It's an SUV that is burgundy colored and has a dreamcatcher hanging below the rearview mirror; both characteristics that Bill had described in their last correspondence.

Behind the wheel sits Bill, wearing a baseball cap and a green parka over a red-and-black flannel shirt. He looks a bit older than he did in the portrait photo on the website. Adam notices this right away, even though the cap covers a good portion of Bill's face.

The driver's side door of the SUV opens at the exact second that the entrance doors slide aside for Adam, and the two men both shudder at the encounter with the icy wind.

At least it's not snowing right now, Adam thinks, but that's a small consolation because it still feels like the wind is going straight through his clothes, skin, and hair.

"Mr. Gray?"

"Just call me Adam. And you must be Bill, right?"

"That's what it says on my birth certificate," he replies with a smile, after which he jogs across the parking lot, holding out his hand.

"I hope you didn't wait too long," he says as Adam shakes it. "I don't live that far away, but my neighbor had parked his tractor in front of my driveway, so I had to wait for him to get off his ass and move it."

"No worries," Adam replies, nodding at the beverages he holds under his arm. "We've only been here for five minutes and took the opportunity to stock up."

Bill nods and glances in the direction of Adam's car.

"I see you've got two girls. They're going to love the place. The animals are always a hit with the young girls. Especially the rabbits and the piglets."

"I can imagine. Actually, that was one of the reasons why I chose your cabin. Getting to feed the animals is pretty exciting for, um ..."

He's just about to say *city slickers*, as the man in the coveralls called them, but then changes it to:

"... city people like us."

Bill lets out a sound that is somewhere between a snort and a laugh.

"Yeah, I guess there aren't a lot of chicken coops in ... Newcrest, was it?"

"Yeah—and no, you won't find many farm animals in our neighborhood."

"Well, then, what do you say we head on up to the cabin so you can meet the little critters?"

"And get warm," Adam adds.

"And get warm," Bill repeats, after which he turns around and starts walking back to the SUV. "You just follow me—and if at any point you're having trouble keeping up, you flash the high beams a few times, okay?"

Adam replies with a nod and a raised thumb. Next, he pulls up the collar of his coat to protect his neck from the piercing wind and runs over to his family in the car.

If you think you're out in the country now, you just wait.

That was the clerk's description of their destination, and when Bill's cabin finally appears at the end of the winding dirt road that has led them up the mountain, in and out through large clusters of snow-covered pines, Adam has to admit that it wasn't an exaggeration.

The cabin is located in a large, crescent-shaped recess. In the summer months it might be a beautiful, grassy valley, but with all the snow right now, it most of all looks like a white lake surrounded by dark trees— and in its middle, the cabin floats like a lost ship.

There are no other houses in sight, and the only sounds are the wind whistling outside the car and the muffled crunch of snow and gravel under the tires.

Inside the car, there are no sounds at all because all four family members sit completely still and stare out the windshield. And all four of them instinctively hold their breath as they study what is going to be their home for the next week.

Rarely has anything filled Adam with such opposing feelings as this sight does. Simultaneously, the cabin looks both *inviting* and *intimidating*. The windows shine with a warm, orange glow and give a wordless promise of a break from the stressful everyday life ... but around them, the grayish wood of the facade is worn from sun and wind, and the roof is heavy with snow that threatens to fall down at any moment and bury the cabin so it merges with the white surface of the valley.

"Somebody is in there," Abby's voice sounds from the back seat.

Adam squints his eyes. She is right, there is a silhouette behind the curtains in one of the cabin's windows—and now, looking closer, he can also see a car. It's parked next to a barn that is located on the right side, a bit drawn back from the cabin.

In front of them, Bill's SUV turns to the side and stops. Then he reaches his arm out of the window and gestures toward the barn.

"What does he want?" Beth asks.

"He wants us to park in there, I think."

Now, almost as a confirmation of those words, Bill gets out of the SUV and runs over to the barn. Once there, he pulls open the door and waves them in.

Like the cabin's windows, the barn is also lit by a warm, orange light. It comes from a row of lamps that hang down from some of the beams out on the sides where the ceiling is lowest.

"Oh, my God! They're so *cute!*"

Chloe's outburst makes Adam jump in his seat, but as soon as his brain decodes the words, the shock transforms into joy.

And the rabbits *are* cute. A small group, lined up neatly behind the cage's wire mesh, stare curiously at the newly arrived guests with small, black eyes.

One of them, a small, white dwarf rabbit with black spots, balances on its hind legs and stretches up, almost as if trying to peek into the back seat of the car, perhaps hoping to spot some treats.

"I thought you'd like them," Adam says. "We're looking after them while we live here."

"It's gonna be so cool!" Chloe exclaims ... but even

though her obvious excitement makes Adam happy, it's her older sister's follow-up that really warms his heart.

"Not bad, Dad," she says softly but sincerely. "Not bad at all."

Even Beth nods with the hint of a smile on her lips.

"Welcome to the hidden paradise of Willowbend," Bill says as they get out of the car. "I see that you've spotted the bunnies. There are also chickens and piglets."

He points toward the other end of the barn where there's a large chicken cage built with wooden posts and wire mesh. Next to it is a pigpen enclosed by a sturdy metal frame. The ground within is covered with a thick layer of straw, and in the middle of the pen is a small, rectangular wooden house that—if it weren't for the feed and water troughs attached to its sides—could easily be mistaken for a child's playhouse.

While Beth and the girls say hello to the animals, Bill grabs Adam's arm and hands him a bunch of keys.

Adam looks at the keychain's pendant and then at Bill's hand.

"Yup, it's a dreamcatcher," Bill says, turning his hand so that Adam can get a better look at the engraving on his ring. "And yes, it's the same one that I've got hanging from the rearview mirror in my car. It's my wife. She has roots in the Ojibwe tribe, and this is one of the ways she holds on to her culture."

A crooked smile forms on his lips, and he lowers his voice to a *just between you and me* whisper.

"Usually, I tell her that I know she's just plastering them all over the place to scare all the other women away and let them know that I'm taken."

He lets out a hoarse chuckle, which Adam can't help but take part in. As it dies out again, Bill grabs his arm once more.

"There are a couple of things you need to know about this place," he says. "First of all, there's absolutely no cell service up here ... but I'm guessing you've already figured that out."

"There were a few frustrated complaints from the back seat on the way up here," Adam confirms. "But that's okay. They were warned in advance. Besides, that was kind of the main goal with this trip; to spend some time together as a family."

"Sounds like a good idea. However, in case of emergency, there is an old landline in the master bedroom inside the cabin. It still works, and my number is on a sticker under the bottom."

"That's good to know."

"The other thing is the animals," Bill continues, bringing Adam with him over to a large cabinet by the wall to the left. "All the feed is stored in here."

He starts opening the doors but freezes when a woman's voice emerges from behind them.

"Perhaps the girls should see this as well?"

Bill and Adam both turn around and are greeted by an elderly woman standing in the barn's doorway, holding an oil lamp in her hand.

Adam recognizes her. It was her silhouette they saw behind the curtains when they arrived.

"Holy crap, Miss Morris," Bill exclaims. "You almost scared the life out of me. Everything's alright up here, I trust?"

The older woman's lips curl into a faint smile, and she nods slowly.

"Fine and dandy, Mr. Tavern."

Adam isn't sure why, but something about the woman makes the hairs on the back of his neck stand up. Then again, maybe he does know. Her black coat, pale skin, and the bun in her hair make her look like a character from a horror movie. The oil lamp doesn't exactly work against that idea either.

"This is Miss Morris. She looks after the place when there aren't any guests."

Adam takes a step forward to shake the woman's hand but changes his mind when he only receives a brief nod from her. A nod that feels as chilly as the breeze coming in from the doorway behind her.

"And you're absolutely right, Miss Morris," Bill continues. "Since it's probably the girls who will be taking care of the animals most of the time, they, of course, should see this as well."

"Abby and Chloe!" Adam calls. "Come over here a sec, will you?"

His daughters, now standing by the piglets, reluctantly let go of the metal railing and walk over to him.

"This is the food for the animals," Bill says, gesturing down to three blue plastic barrels standing at the bottom of the cabinet. "It's easy enough because they're in the same order as the cages; bunnies, chick ens, pigs."

He moves his hand up to a shelf at the top of the cabinet. From it, he picks up a laminated piece of paper and turns it toward them.

"On this you can see when to feed them and how much. So ... can anyone tell me when it's time to feed the chickens again?"

Behind Adam, Chloe's hand cautiously rises in the air, and Bill gives her a *go-ahead* nod.

"Tomorrow morning?"

Bill winks at her and smiles before returning the paper to the shelf.

"I think the animals are in good hands," he says. "Don't you agree, Miss Morris?"

"I certainly do."

"Good. Then how about we take a look at where you're going to sleep for the next seven days?"

The other members of his family answer with a unanimous *sure*, but Adam says nothing. His attention is caught by the sensation of something touching his back.

It's Beth's hand, gently gliding over it. It's brief but undoubtedly a caress.

The first one in a long time.

"So, what's the verdict?" Bill asks.

"It's a very nice place you've got here."

That is an understatement. Adam finds the cabin nothing short of wonderful—and his wife's eyes tell him that he isn't the only one.

In particular, he is blown away by the contrast. Because stepping over the threshold really felt like stepping into another world. The obvious difference is, of course, the temperature; the harsh cold outside versus the enveloping heat inside the cabin. But it's more than that. Far more.

Out in the rugged mountain landscape, the world was basically reduced to two colors, black and white, but inside, in the warm living room of the cabin, shades of brown, red, and gold are woven together to create a cozy and welcoming atmosphere.

The crucial element of this effect is of course the fireplace that is built into the back wall of the living room. Its crackling flames cast dancing shadows on the dark brown wood paneling of the walls, and the deep orange light of the fire softens the edges of everything it touches.

On the left side, the kitchen lies in extension of the living room, separated only by a half wall with built-in shelves filled with rustic jars and various small decorative items.

From one of the jars, Bill picks up a small key and holds it out for everyone to see.

"Most likely you won't need it, but this is the key to

our reserve supply in case your food should run out. You'll find it behind the cabin, about halfway down in the backyard. A rusty metal hatch with a padlock, hard to miss. Originally, it was a bomb shelter, I think. But now we just use it to store food. It's not Michelin quality, but it'll keep you alive in the event of a snowstorm."

Adam and Beth exchange a glance, and Bill's hand immediately goes up.

"I'm not trying to scare you," he says. "And as I said, it's very unlikely that you'll need it. I'm just telling you so you don't need to get nervous if it starts snowing for real."

Snowing for real? Adam repeats in his thoughts, letting his gaze drift out onto the white landscape outside the window. *Then what do you call this?*

"Well, guess that's it," Bill says as he drops the key back into the jar. "Then Miss Morris and I will get going so you can get to know the place on your own."

"I'll walk you out," Adam replies. "I have to get our things from the car anyway."

Outside, the sun is setting behind the peaks of the mountains, and as it gradually vanishes, so does the sense of feeling in Adam's fingers. The cold enters them, paralyzes them so that he is hardly able to feel it when he shakes Bill's hand for the last time.

And when he—after seeing Bill and Miss Morris drive down the mountain and disappear from sight among a cluster of snowy pines—opens the trunk of his car and starts to carry suitcases, bags, and boxes into the cabin, his fingers are practically numb.

It's cold up here. Colder than anything he remembers having experienced before.

An hour later, he has forgotten all about the cold. Because by then, he is sitting in an armchair in front of the fireplace, watching his daughters on the couch as they work together to solve a *crossword* puzzle. Behind them, on the other side of the half wall between the kitchen and the living room, Beth stands. She is preparing dinner ... and she's humming softly while doing it.

This doesn't mean that all their problems have magically gone away, of course not. But it's a damned good start, and Adam feels increasingly happier that he insisted on them going on this vacation. A break from the daily grind will do them good.

Some peace and quiet.

No sooner has this thought manifested in his head than it is torn apart again by a series of intense screeching sounds that erupt outside.

"What *is* that?" Chloe asks.

Adam glances at Beth, who answers with a shrug and a slightly worried grimace.

"The chickens?" Adam says, mostly to himself. Then he nods and elaborates with a more confident tone of voice: "It's probably just the chickens who got upset by something. Maybe the piglets are making fun of them."

He added that last sentence for Chloe's sake. To calm her nine-year-old mind. It doesn't seem to work very well, though ... and to be honest, he's not too fond of the racket either. Because the chickens keep squawking loudly, and underneath their screeches there is also something else. Something that sounds like hammering.

"Maybe you should go out there and check," Beth suggests.

"Yeah, sure," Adam says, after which he gets up from the armchair and walks to the front door. Before opening it, he glances back at the fireplace—and at the fire poker hanging on a stand next to it. In the end, however, he decides that bringing it would do more harm than good. Chloe isn't stupid. She would figure out what he was planning to use it for, and it would only make her even more anxious if she saw him bring an improvised weapon.

Outside, the noise is far louder. It reverberates in the snowy driveway, and it doesn't take him many seconds to decide that his assumption was correct: The sound is coming from the barn. And it's definitely the chickens.

At least the hysterical squawking is. He's still not sure about the knocking sounds.

"What on Earth is up with you guys?"

Adam isn't in the habit of talking out loud to himself. In fact, he's not sure he's ever done it before. But he hasn't exactly been in a situation like this before either. Alone, high up on a mountain in the middle of nowhere, on his way to investigate some scary noises while surrounded by a rough landscape that the moonlight has given an eerie, bluish morgue glow.

Oh, come on. You're getting yourself worked up over nothing. You'll be laughing about this tomorrow.

Perhaps. But that doesn't change the fact that his feet don't want to carry him over to the barn door. And that he doesn't want to force them to.

He does so anyway and walks across the driveway with the snow creaking and groaning ominously under his boots.

The handle is freezing cold when he grabs it with both hands and pulls. Above him, the wheels of the metal rail screech and the door slides aside, gradually unfolding a large fan of moonlight onto the concrete floor of the barn.

The first thing he notices is the puddle. It's lying on the floor a bit to the right of the car, which may be the reason why, for a split second, he thinks that it's an oil spill.

But it's not oil. It's blood. A viscous, sticky pool of it. Like a drip painting, as abstract as it is macabre.

And—he realizes to his horror—the eerie pool of blood next to the car may be the largest, but it's not the only one. In several places on the floor there are smaller puddles. Near one of these, there is also a dark red stain on the wall, roughly eight inches above floor level.

Deep down, Adam knows he has to do something. He has to *act*. But he can't. His body, his brain ... nothing obeys. It's as if he has been overloaded with sensory impressions. The screeches of the animals, the pounding sounds, the sight of the blood, *the smell* of the blood, he can't—

Something shoots out from the shadows at the far end of the barn and sprints across the floor in his direction. Instinctively, he tries to jump to the side, but his state of shock slows him down and he doesn't have time to dodge before the headless chicken collides with his legs and a spray of fresh blood shoots out from its open throat. It hits his pants, his coat, his hands.

He staggers backward as the headless chicken changes direction and sprints to the left until the wall stops it with a thump. Now, it lies on the floor, completely still.

"What the hell ... what the hell ... what the hell," Adam mumbles as he alternately stares at the chicken's dead body and down at his bloodstained clothes. Neither makes sense to him.

When the inevitable comprehension finally comes, it hits his body first. His left hand, almost on its own, starts frantically scrubbing at the bloodstain on his sleeve. Harder and harder until his palm feels scorching hot.

After his hand's motor reflex, his brain awakens. It happens abruptly, as if a torch is lit inside his mind, illuminating an old piece of information from his school years. A knowledge that has remained hidden in the archives of his memory for decades.

Sometimes, when a chicken is beheaded, the vestibular nerve and some of its motor functions can still remain active. This enables it to run around for a while without a head.

A natural phenomenon. He even has a faint recollection of watching a video of it in class. But it's one thing to see it on a screen, quite another to see it in real life. Hell, it *ran into* him. Rammed into his legs.

With hesitant steps, he approaches the dead chicken and crouches down in front of it. He doesn't want to touch it, but he has to be sure. Therefore, he stretches out a quivering finger and pokes at one of its wings, gently at first, then a little harder.

No reaction. Thank God.

He pulls in a deep breath, holds the air inside his lungs for a moment, and then lets it out again in a long, hissing sigh—and as the sound of it hits his own ears, he realizes something:

It's almost completely quiet in here now. The chickens no longer squawk, and the banging sounds are gone as well.

He gets up, walks over to the wall, and flips the light switch. Along the wooden beams at the sides of the barn, the lamps turn on, bathing the space in a warm, orange glow.

The light is more than welcome. It gives him the courage to move down to the back of the barn.

To the chicken cage.

His hope is to have the best-case scenario con-firmed. To find a hole in the fence or a loose board in the back wall of the barn that would allow a fox or another predator to enter. Because that has to be the explanation, right? Some predator getting its claws on a chicken and ripping its head off before getting scared away by the racket of the other animals. What else could it be?

This is what Adam thinks as he stops and lets his gaze wander around the chicken cage. The wire mesh is fastened in all the right places. There are no loose staples and no visible openings. All the beams and boards look steady, and it doesn't seem like more than the one chicken is missing. The others are strutting around in there, no longer caring about the massacre that has just taken place. If there was an exit, they would've tried to escape during the commotion, right? However, there is nothing at all to indicate—

Wait. There, in the shadows beneath the nesting boxes, lies a small pile of something white on top of the sawdust that makes up the floor of the cage.

He squints his eyes. Snow. Definitely. And if there is snow, there must also be an opening where it has entered.

He opens the door to the cage, edges his way past a couple of confused chickens, and walks over to the nesting boxes, where he bends down.

He was right. A couple of feet above the floor,

there is a loose board in the back wall. It's not a very large gap, but presumably enough for a fox or a mink.

Relieved—more than he likes to admit—he pulls the board back into place and leaves the chicken cage. Next, he walks over to the cabinet where the animal feed is stored. He is pretty sure that he saw a roll of plastic bags in there earlier.

Yup, on the second highest shelf is a roll of large garbage bags. He takes one and brings it with him over to the headless chicken.

A wave of nausea rolls up his throat as he grabs the dead animal and lifts it up. It's the feathers that are the worst. The way they feel soft and spongy against his fingers. As if they're moist. *Soaked.*

Once the chicken has been packed away safely and the bag closed with a double knot, he throws it in the garbage container outside. Then he walks around the cabin until he reaches the kitchen window on the other side.

Beth is standing in there, bent over in front of the stove, and she jolts as he knocks gently on the window. She spins around, spots him, and her lips form a swear word.

He points down to the window handle, which she reluctantly opens.

"What do you think you're doing?" she whispers out through the crack between the frame and the window-pane. "You scared me."

"I need your help out in the barn," Adam replies. "And don't say anything to the girls, okay?"

Beth casts a glance into the living room, where the girls are still sitting on the couch, and then back at him.

"Can't it wait? The food is almost ready, and—"

"Beth!" he interrupts, gesturing down to his pants. "Look at me!"

For a split second she looks angry, as though she's about to slam the window shut and turn her back on him, but then she sees it. His pants. His coat. The bloodstains.

"What the heck happened to you?" she stammers.

"It was one of the chickens. Its head was bitten off. Probably a fox or something. I've removed the body, but there's still a lot of blood on the floor out there. I'd like to get rid of it before the girls see it."

"Okay, I ... I'll get a bucket and some soapy water. I think I saw a mop in the closet."

"Good. And bring me a pair of clean pants too, okay?"

Beth nods, still with a look of confusion on her face. Then she closes the window and disappears into the cabin to find the items.

Meanwhile, Adam heads back to the barn and waits for her. And while he is standing there, he replays the entire scenario in his head again; the panicked chickens, the loud banging, the darkness of the barn, the pool of blood, and the headless chicken that emerged from the shadows and torpedoed his legs.

He's missing something. Some detail that he can sense is there but that he can't get a grip on. Something he registered peripherally, but not—

Suddenly, it breaks through to the surface. In a movement so abrupt that he almost loses his balance, he spins around and sprints out to the garbage container. He tears open the lid, grabs the bag with the dead chicken, tears a hole in the plastic … and feels a chill move over his neck.

It's a clean cut. Whatever being separated the chicken's head from its neck wasn't a fox or a similar predator. If it were, there would've been bite marks and strands of shredded flesh on the neck.

But there isn't. There is only one single cut. Straight and completely clean.

December 2nd

◦◦◦

Beth

Bethany Gray is *not* a morning person. It's not that she sleeps in, because she rarely does. In fact, she typically wakes up an hour before she needs to. However, her eyes being open doesn't mean that her heart and arms are. Because Beth is almost always grumpy in the early hours. Her world doesn't gain color until she has had a shower and a cup of coffee. Before that, everything is gloomy and gray. Sometimes pitch black.

This also applies to her husband. There are times when she'll lie there, staring at him, without feeling anything but a profound, gray emptiness.

Not hate, not anger, just emptiness.

A close friend once suggested that she might be suffering from mild depression, and that diagnosis, albeit unconfirmed, makes sense to Beth. Especially since the feeling typically disappears once the day really starts.

Over the last six months, however, the feeling has been more stubborn. It has dug its claws into her from the morning and held on. Sometimes she has found herself sitting at the table during dinner, staring at Adam with the same feeling of emptiness in her heart.

And yes, she has also considered whether he could be the cause.

On this, their first morning in the cabin, though, the world isn't gray. It's bright and inviting. Even despite the fact that she spent much of her first evening of vacation mopping up blood in the barn, thanks to some stupid fox that couldn't keep its paws to itself.

Part of the reason for Beth's good mood is the view of the mountains, which was the first thing her eyes met when she opened them. Another part is the sounds coming from downstairs.

Laughter. The rattle of plates. Adam and the girls are up, and they're enjoying themselves.

She stretches her body and swings her legs over the edge of the bed. The carpet feels soft and warm against her bare toes.

After getting up, she pulls on her clothes—a pair of jeans and a loose-fitting sweater. Once she has done so, she takes a final look at the mountain landscape before leaving the bedroom and heading downstairs.

"Looks like someone is out to score some points today," she says as she comes down the stairs and catches sight of the kitchen.

Adam and Chloe, both standing in front of the stove, look up and smile at her.

"Pancakes," Adam says, pointing his spatula down at the pan on the stove. He then turns the spatula toward Chloe, who after a moment of confusion gestures toward the stove, saying:

"And bacon and eggs!"

"Yum!" Beth says as she walks over to the dining table, which Abby is busy setting. "Good morning, sweetie. How was your first night in the cabin? Did your little sister chat all night, or did you manage to get some sleep?"

"Nah, it was okay. She did blabber for a while, but ... it was okay."

Two times 'it was okay,' Beth thinks. *In teen language, this must mean that she is really enjoying herself.*

"Your timing is excellent," Adam says from the kitchen. "The food is done now, so feel free to take a seat."

Beth and Abby do just that—and as soon as they're seated, Adam comes over with a plateful of steaming hot pancakes, which he places in the middle of the table. Only now, as he puts them down, does Beth realize that he is wearing an apron. A pretty ugly one.

"Where did you find *that*?" she asks, pointing.

"Oh, this old thing?" he says, pulling at the edges so the design—a bulldog wearing a Santa hat and the text *WHO LET THE HO'S OUT?*—is easier to see. "I found it in one of the drawers out in the utility room, and since it's the second of December today, I figured, why not?"

Beth shrugs her shoulders and smiles.

Once the rest of the meal is set out, the remaining two take their seats at the table and start helping themselves. The food is delicious, and the atmosphere is merry. Even Abby joins in on the conversation, and Beth only catches her rolling her eyes once. And given that it's in response to one of her dad's lame jokes (*Why do Christmas trees suck at sewing? They keep dropping their needles*), it's entirely forgivable.

As the plates are emptied and the stomachs filled, a pleasant silence falls over them all. This also lingers as they start to clean up after breakfast.

At one point, though, the silence is broken when Chloe suddenly stops in front of one of the windows facing the driveway.

"What is that?"

"What's what?"

"That thing, over by the barn," Chloe says, pointing as best she can with a stack of dirty plates in her hands. "On the barn door."

Instinctively, Beth's gaze finds Adam's face.

Didn't we get it all? she asks without words.

I ... I think so, his eyes answer.

"It kind of looks like a ... Christmas stocking," Chloe says, after which she glances back and forth between her parents.

"Don't look at us," Adam says, holding his hands up in front of him.

Chloe squints her eyes. Then her gaze shifts to her older sister.

"As if," Abby hums.

"But if it's not you guys," Chloe says, "then who?"

Once again, Beth's eyes wander to Adam, but there is no help to be had. He just shrugs, looking precisely as confused as she feels.

"Bill?" she suggests, receiving another shrug before Adam answers.

"I mean, he didn't really strike me as the type to play Secret Santa, but it's not like I have a better idea, so ... maybe?"

"Can we go out and see what's in it?" Chloe asks.

"Maybe we should ..." Beth begins, but the pleading look in Chloe's eyes overpowers her before she reaches the end of the sentence. She sighs and nods. "Okay, fine."

Chloe puts the stack of plates on the windowsill and throws a celebratory punch into the air.

"Yes! Thanks, Mom."

"You're welcome, sweetie."

"What ... is it?"

The disappointment in Chloe's voice is palpable.

Frankly, though, it's understandable. She probably expected to find something a little more fun in the dirty—and half-frozen—Christmas stocking hanging on a rusty nail on the barn door. So did Beth.

And that Chloe has no idea what the small, square object in her hand is doesn't come as a surprise either. Few kids of her generation would.

"It's a slide," Adam says, putting out his hand, palm facing up.

Chloe gives him the slide, and he holds it up against the light for a moment, squinting his eyes. Then he shakes his head and hands it to Beth as he continues his explanation to Chloe.

"A slide is a kind of photograph. In the old days, there were these projectors that could be used to enlarge the images and display them on a screen using light."

"A screen? Like a TV?"

"Well, more like the screens you'd find in a movie theater. These were more for home use, though. You'd use them for showing your vacation photos to the whole family at once. Stuff like that."

As he speaks, Beth studies the slide more closely, but the image is blurry, making it difficult to discern the details.

"It ... could be the ridge behind us," she says after a while.

"Can I see?" Adam asks.

She hands him the slide, and he holds it up against the light once more. Afterward he looks at the peaks of the mountains towering above them and nods.

"You know what? I think you're right. And if it's the mountain ridge, then ... *that* little spot there would be the cabin."

He points with one hand while holding up the slide with the other so Beth and the girls can see the dark spot.

"Maybe it's some kind of game," Abby suggests. "A treasure hunt or something like that?"

Adam tilts his head slightly and studies the small image one more time. Then he grimaces.

"It sure isn't much to go by."

"I know," Abby says. "But maybe there'll be something new tomorrow. Another clue."

Adam and Beth exchange a glance, and she can read in his eyes that he feels torn about this too. If it's a treasure hunt, fine. Maybe even a really good idea that Bill or Miss Morris came up with. But why didn't any of them mention it then?

Maybe you're still a little spooked by the thing with the chicken yesterday, she says to herself. *After all, this is just a Christmas stocking. Hardly anything to get worked up about, right?*

"I say we wait and see if there's something new in the stocking tomorrow," she says and smiles at her daughters. "In the meantime, since you're already dressed for the cold, why don't the two of you make the most of it and build a snowman together? Then I'll have some hot cocoa ready for you when you come in. How does that sound?"

While asking the question, she makes eye contact with Abby, hoping that she can persuade her to do it for her little sister's sake, even if she doesn't really want to. However, this turns out to be unnecessary because Abby takes the lead all by herself. She bends down, makes a snowball, and throws it at Chloe.

And that's all it takes. The game is on, and the parents can stroll back to the cabin and clean up after breakfast in peace and quiet.

"We call him the Adorable Snowman," Chloe proclaims.

"Not to be mistaken for his cousin, the Abominable Snowman," Abby adds.

With those words, both girls step aside and reveal their masterpiece; a snowman whose round head is adorned with gray eyes of pebbles and a crooked nose made with a half-eaten carrot that they found in the rabbit cage. His mouth is crafted with three small twigs, and his arms consist of two branches that the girls—which Beth finds rather creative—have bent midway so that it appears as if the snowman is standing with his hands resting on his hips.

"Well, if nothing else, he certainly is ... unique," says Adam, who has also been called out for the big reveal.

"Ha ha, Dad. Very funny," Chloe replies, sticking out her tongue.

"I think it's gorgeous, girls ... sorry, *he* is gorgeous."

"Thanks, Mom."

As such, it's not a lie. Beth actually thinks her daughters have achieved quite a work of art. Especially since she was unsure whether they would even finish it today, given that they took a long break from the project around noon and didn't go out again until late afternoon. But they did get it done, and with a fine result. She's particularly fond of Abby's idea of dressing the snowman in Adam's hideous Christmas apron from this morning. It's the perfect finishing touch.

"Well," Adam says, rubbing his hands together. "How about we feed the animals and then head inside? You still owe me a rematch after that card game, remember?"

"Can the snowman keep the apron, or do we have to take it inside?" Chloe asks.

Adam looks at Beth, who shrugs her shoulders and nods.

"I don't see the harm in letting him keep it for a day or two."

The girls exchange a smile and then head over to the barn with their dad. Beth starts walking too but then hesitates and stops when she discovers that one of the snowman's eyes has come loose.

"That's more like it," she whispers as she pushes the small gray pebble back into place.

She turns around and starts walking toward the barn for the second time ... but once again, she hesitates as she registers something out of the corner of her eye.

About a hundred yards up the mountainside— could be more, could be less; estimating distances isn't her greatest talent—there is a plateau surrounded by tall pine trees. On it, a vehicle is parked, a black snowmobile, and behind its handlebars sits a man in a white snowsuit.

What is he doing all the way up there? Beth thinks, bringing her hand up to her forehead to shield her eyes from the light so she can see better.

Right at that moment, the headlights turn on and the snowmobile reverses a bit before turning in toward the mountain and disappearing out of sight behind the edge of the plateau. It seems rushed, almost clumsy. Like a startled animal hurrying away.

Shortly after, it briefly appears a little further down in between two clusters of trees, but it's quickly gone again. The only additional detail Beth manages to catch is that the glass cover on one of the taillights is missing, so it glows white while the other glows red.

She stays for a moment longer, her gaze flickering across the snowy mountainside, hoping to catch another glimpse of the vehicle. She doesn't, but with each passing second, it also feels less important.

With a shrug, Beth accepts her defeat and turns her back on the mountain. It's probably time for her to head inside anyway if she wants to get some snacks ready for the card game before Adam and the girls finish up in the barn.

December 3rd

⸛

Abby

"Abby? Are you awake?"

"Does it look like I'm awake, Chloe?"

"I can't sleep anymore."

"And that's my problem because ...?"

"Come on, Abby. Please. I'm bored."

Reluctantly, Abby opens her eyes and is met with the blurry outline of her little sister's body, sharply contrasted by the pale daylight streaming in through the window behind her.

"Chloe, we're on *vacation*."

"I know, but I can't sleep anymore, and I want to see if there's anything in the Christmas stocking today. And Mom said I have to take you with me if I go outside before they get up."

Abby rubs her face and yawns loudly while she contemplates how much she actually likes her little sister. A bit less than usual at this moment, that's for sure ,,, but still enough to give in.

"Oh, Chloe, you're so annoying," she groans and sits up in bed. "Do you know that?"

"Of course," Chloe replies. "You tell me all the time. But thanks."

"Yeah, yeah. Whatever."

Once up and dressed, Abby goes down to the kitchen with her little sister, where she grabs a juice box from the fridge and brings it with her outside. It's not exactly a nutritious breakfast, but it's better than nothing, and she has to get something in her stomach. Besides, she can always find something better when they get back in. It shouldn't take long to check the stupid stocking.

Stepping out the door almost makes her change her mind and jump back under the covers. Because it's cold this morning. So cold that it feels like the wind is blowing through her clothes, skin, and flesh, reaching all the way into her bones.

The Christmas stocking still hangs in the same spot as the day before; on a rusty nail in the middle of the barn door. Before she puts her hand into it, Abby touches the outside. Not that it's of much help. The fabric is so stiff from the cold that she can't tell if there's anything inside it or not. There is no way around it. She'll just have to get it over with and put her hand into the stocking.

For a moment, that conclusion fills her with a

strange uneasiness and makes her hesitate. Not for long, of course, because she has an audience, and she doesn't want to lose face in front of her little sister.

Carefully, she moves her hand down past the fuzzy white edge at the top of the stocking and down toward the bottom. The uneven—and icy—structure of the fabric prickles against her fingers. It feels as if the entire inside is coated with tiny ice crystals.

"Is there anything in it?" Chloe asks with a hopeful, almost begging tone in her voice.

"Just a sec, I need to get all the way down to … whoa, wait." She hesitates and then purses her lips into a smile. "I do believe we've got another slide."

She pulls her hand up and shows the slide to Chloe, who immediately snatches it from her. After a moment's inspection, however, she hands it back, clearly disappointed.

"Man, it's just the same as yesterday. The cabin and the mountains."

Abby holds the small image up in front of her face and tilts it from side to side a couple of times. Then she shakes her head.

"Not exactly. This one is closer."

"What do you mean?"

"Look at this part," Abby says, running a finger along one edge of the image. "Yesterday you could see the trees at the point where those two mountains meet. Today, they're out of the frame. The photographer was closer this time."

"Oh, maybe it'll get a bit closer every day until we can see where the treasure is hidden," Chloe suggests.

"That would be pretty cool, huh?" Abby says, smiling, even though there's a part of her that feels a brief sting of unease again.

"Do you want to try and see if we can find him?"

"Find who?"

"Our Secret Santa, of course," Chloe says, sighing as if it's awfully draining having to explain everything in such detail to her dopey big sister.

Surprised that she hasn't had that thought herself, Abby lets her gaze drift down to the ground in front of the barn door.

No footprints? How can that be? It did snow a bit last night, but not nearly enough to cover—

A new observation breaks her stream of thought. Because there *is* a track, she realizes. It's just not footprints, but rather a much wider track, about three and a half feet from edge to edge, which runs from the barn door out to the trees on the east side.

Someone has been walking there, dragging something behind them to cover their tracks. Something that digs just deep enough into the surface of the snow to loosen it and spread it out.

"If we do it, it's on two conditions," she says. "First of all, we'll do it later, because I'm cold and I'm hungry. Secondly, we don't say a word about it to Mom and Dad. We just tell them that we're going out to collect pinecones or something. Deal?"

Chloe glances back at the cabin and makes a strained swallowing motion. Then she nods.

"Deal."

"Maybe we should just give up and go home."

Chloe's voice sounds fragile. Almost like she has trouble squeezing out the words.

Abby knows why. Chloe is scared. The sounds of the forest are starting to get under her skin: The snow crunching under their feet. The remote flapping of bird wings and branches breaking. The wind's constant whispering in the treetops.

Truth be told, Abby isn't exactly immune to it either. But now they've followed that stupid track this far, and she intends to find out where it leads to. Therefore, she gives her little sister a light pat on the back and says:

"Nah, let's keep going. We're close, I think."

At least it's still early afternoon, so they have plenty of time to get home before darkness falls. Even Abby would set the limit there. This forest at night? That would be a firm no.

The track is a bit narrower now that they're some distance into the forest, but it's still the same weird furrow, as if someone has dragged a wide leaf rake behind them.

Or perhaps a bundle of thin branches? That is

probably more likely, she concludes.

Whatever it is, there can be no doubt about the purpose. Their Secret Santa intends to remain secret.

A sound, somewhere further up the mountainside, interrupts her thoughts. It's a faint whistle—gone again so quickly that she would have doubted that she actually heard it if her little sister hadn't also stopped and glanced around.

"What was that?" Chloe asks.

"Just a bird," Abby replies, though the answer to the same question is different inside her head. Because it didn't really sound like a bird's chirp, did it? It sounded like a person whistling.

Would you relax? It's just Chloe's edginess that's rubbing off on you.

Maybe. But that doesn't change the fact that the tiny seed of doubt has been sown in her mind ... and it's growing, much faster than she'd prefer.

"I'd like to go back to the cabin now, Abby."

Abby stops and lets her gaze drift along the track, which takes a sharp turn about twenty-five yards further on before continuing up a slope and disappearing from sight.

"Okay, what do you say we follow the track up there?" she says and points. "And if we can't see where it ends from there, we'll turn back."

Chloe hesitates, long enough for Abby to feel a twinge of guilt, but then finally nods.

"Good, then let's do that," Abby says, offering her a hand. "And don't worry, I've got your back."

Chloe takes her hand and lets herself be led. She almost immediately has to let go of it again, though, as the slope is both steep and slippery.

"Use the trees for support," Abby says, demonstrating by wrapping her arms around a tree trunk. "Hug a tree."

Chloe rolls her eyes but still follows the advice and leans on trunks and branches as she climbs the slope.

Abby reaches the top first, but much to her disappointment, the track's mystery remains unsolved as it continues over a wide depression, which could be a path or a narrow road, and from there into a new forest area.

Damn it.

She starts to turn around to tell her little sister the discouraging news, but then stops dead in her tracks.

A movement. A dark silhouette who was there for a split second and then disappeared behind one of the tree trunks.

They're not alone. There is someone in the forest. Someone who is keeping an eye on them.

She almost screams as something brushes against her leg. Spinning around on her heels, she sees Chloe kneeling on the ground, reaching out a hand.

"Hello! I asked if you could help me up!"

For a moment, Abby just stares at her blankly, unable to understand what it is she wants her to do.

Then the words finally sink in, and she kneels next to Chloe.

"It's not worth it," she says, "so crawl back down. The track just continues, so I say we go home now."

Chloe stares at her warily.

"But I'm not really scared anymore, so it's okay with me if we—"

"We're going back to the cabin now, Chloe. I'm also pretty cold."

Another moment of skeptical staring, then Chloe shrugs and starts crawling down the slope again.

December 4th

Chloe

It's 1:46 p.m. on their fourth day at the cabin, and Chloe is disappointed. On several levels.

The first letdown was the Christmas stocking this morning. In it was yet another dumb slide, which also showed the cabin, just a little closer and from the other side. She's starting to doubt that they'll even get all the clues before the vacation is over.

The second disappointment of the day is her big sister. Her *boring* big sister, who didn't want to play the old Monopoly game that Chloe found in one of the cupboards, and who also didn't want to go out in the backyard because she needed to *kick back and recharge a bit*. As if Abby has anything to be stressed about! She is popular at school, she has plenty of friends, and she doesn't even have any real chores at home.

"She just wants to seem more grown up than she is,"

Chloe mumbles and lifts Bumbleball up so that its soft fur touches her cheek.

Bumbleball is her favorite bunny among the five who live in the cage out in the barn. It's curious by nature, it likes to cuddle, and it's insanely cute with its black-and-white spotted fur, which makes it look like a soccer ball. The latter is also the reason why she named it Bumbleball.

In the absence of her older sister, Bumbleball has been given the honor of acting as Chloe's confidant today. Thus, it must listen to her troubles. That doesn't seem to bother it, though. It sits comfortably in her arms, softly twitching its nose with half-closed eyes.

"What do you think I should do today?" Chloe whispers.

The rabbit doesn't respond. It just turns its head away from her and looks down at the hatch of the cage as if it wants to ask her to put it—

Wait a minute. Maybe the bunny has just answered her question after all. Not on purpose, of course, but still. Because there is another hatch, out in the back-yard. The one that Bill told them about.

Chloe has stared at that hatch several times. She knows that Bill said it just leads down to a room where they store extra food ... but there could be other stuff down there too, right?

Opening that hatch would be exciting. Opening it by herself, without saying anything to Mom and Dad and Abby, would be even more exciting. And she knows where the key is.

Chloe ponders for a moment, after which she glances back over her shoulder, gives Bumbleball one last hug, and puts it back in its cage.

Chloe walks slowly on the tips of her toes, but the living room, like the rest of the cabin, has wooden floors, and the planks creak treacherously underneath her feet. Behind the half wall of the kitchen, her mom turns around.

"Hi, sweetie. Did you have fun with the animals?"

"Yeah, I, um ... I'm going back out in a minute, if that's okay. Just need to get warm."

For a fleeting moment, her mom squints her eyes as if somehow able to sense that her daughter is up to no good. Then she smiles and nods toward the fireplace.

"If you're cold, it's warmer over there."

Chloe looks at the fireplace and then down at the shelf in the half wall where the jar holding the key is.

"It's okay. I'd rather be here with you."

Her mom's eyes widen. Then she smiles.

"That was a very nice thing to say."

Chloe replies with an awkward smile, hoping it will take the focus away from the reddish hue that the lie gives her face. Her cheeks feel burning hot. So does her neck.

For what feels like an eternity, her mom keeps staring at her, and with each passing second, Chloe's doubt grows until she is convinced that she has been exposed.

But then, completely calm and undramatic, her mom shrugs her shoulders and turns around.

Only as she lets the air out between her dry lips with an unexpected sigh does Chloe realize that she has been holding her breath for a long time. Long enough to feel a bit dizzy. She doesn't have time to worry about that, though, because now is the time to act.

With that in mind, she takes an extra look around the living room behind her. Her dad is still lying on the couch with his eyes closed, dried out drool on his cheek and an open book resting on his chest. Good. Behind him is the stairway up to the upper floor where Abby is. And the steps creak like crazy, so even if she were to come down, Chloe would get a heads-up ahead of time.

Okay. This is it.

She leans forward and supports the elbow of her left arm on the top edge of the half wall while her right hand feels its way over the objects on the shelf. She locates the jar, slides her hand into it, and grabs the key.

At that very moment, her mom turns around, holding two wet hands up in front of her.

"Would you mind handing me the dish towel? I hung it to dry on the chair behind you."

Chloe looks at her mom's hands and then at the chair where the dish towel hangs. And while she does this, her quivering right hand transports the key from the jar up to the pocket of her jeans.

"Yeah, of course, Mom," she says, after which she grabs the towel and hands it to her mom.

"Thanks, sweetie. You're an angel."

Chloe doesn't answer that.

Not only is the padlock old and rusty, it's also covered in a thin—but hard—layer of ice and snow, which Chloe has to break off in small pieces before she can insert the key.

At least the lock only protests briefly before it gives in and the shackle pops open with a click.

With fingers shaking, partly due to the cold, partly due to the excitement, she removes the padlock and grabs the handle of the hatch.

The hinges squeak as she pulls, and gradually, what was once a bomb shelter is filled by daylight.

She stares down the narrow staircase that leads to the concrete floor at the bottom of the small room. The walls are also made of concrete, gray and dull with sporadic patches of humidity that look like abstract paintings from the world's least inspired artist.

Along the walls run rusty metal shelves, heavily loaded with supplies of canned food, dried fruit, and water bottles, all covered in dust and cobwebs. There are also a couple of oil lamps of the same type as the one Miss Morris had when she came out to the barn.

With hesitant steps, Chloe walks down the narrow staircase. The steps creak under her weight, but they seem stable enough.

Halfway down, it hits her. A heavy, nauseating smell of mold and ... time. That's the best way she can describe it. It smells old. The way their granddad's basement smelled when it was flooded.

She pulls up her scarf, covering her mouth. It takes the edge off.

Reaching the floor, she stops and lets her gaze drift over the shelves once more. This time she notices something that she didn't spot before.

The ... thing is on the top shelf by the back wall. If possible, it's even more covered in dust and cobwebs than the cans are. It sort of looks like an old-fashioned camera, just bigger.

She walks over to the shelf and stands on her toes so that she can reach the device. As she touches it, she sets some of the threads of a cobweb stretched between the device and the wall in motion, and a disgusting, light brown spider darts across it before disappearing into the shadows under the ceiling. It doesn't touch her, doesn't even come near her ... but it still feels like it does. In fact, her brain does her the dubious favor of telling her how it would feel if it had crawled over the skin of her neck instead of the wall.

She shakes off a chill and makes another attempt. This time with more success. She gets a hold of the device and pulls it down.

It has a lens, but it's not a camera. It can't be. It's far too big and clumsy. Besides, it has a power cable—and that would make it nearly impossible to take pictures outside.

Could it be some kind of projector? Like the ones they use in movie theaters, or ... wait a minute. Could it be one of those things that her dad told them about? A machine that can show the slides?

She wipes dust off the lens with her sleeve and lifts the device up in front of her face so she can examine it more closely. However, she has hardly focused her gaze on the curved glass dome before she freezes.

On the left side of the lens is a small square of light. It's the reflection of daylight from the entrance behind her, above the stairs, where she herself entered.

And in the middle of the square of light is an outline. The silhouette of a human being.

With a new sensation of spider legs crawling over her neck, she turns around and fixes her gaze on the only exit from this reeking concrete prison.

For a split second, her brain remains on high alert, and the silhouette becomes all the things she fears the most; a vampire, a monster, an evil man.

But then the monster opens its mouth and speaks ... in Abby's voice.

"What the hell are you doing, Chloe? Did Mom and Dad say you could go down here?"

"A-Abby, I ..." Chloe's lips continue to move, but no words come out. She probably looks like a fish in an aquarium.

"Seriously, Chloe," Abby continues. "Mom is gonna freak if she finds out about this. You've got to come up. Now."

Chloe looks down at the device in her hands and then up at her older sister.

"But I found this. I think it's for the pictures from the stocking."

Abby stares at her while her face works its way through a variety of different emotions. Confusion, reflection, hesitation, doubt, and finally determination.

"We ... found it over in the barn," she says. "Understood?"

Chloe's heart sinks a little. This is the second time in less than twenty-four hours that Abby has asked her to lie to her parents—and Chloe doesn't like to lie.

On the other hand, she was the one who took the key and snuck down here in the first place.

"I mean it, Chloe," Abby says. "We can't tell them that you found it down here because then I guarantee that they won't let us see the slides. And I don't know about you, but I really want to see them."

"Me too," Chloe stammers.

"Good. Then hurry and bring it up here. And don't forget where we found it."

"In the barn," Chloe says.

"In the barn," Abby repeats.

Even the sounds somehow seem old-fashioned to Chloe's ears. The way the machine is constantly humming and creaking and clicking. As if it has lived a really long life and is complaining about it.

Since they don't have a real projection screen, her dad has drawn the curtains on the window in the living room so they can use them as a background. They aren't entirely white, more like sand-colored, but at least the fabric is fairly free of wrinkles and folds.

"Alright, let's see if it still works," her dad says as he pushes a small drawer into the side of the projector. In the drawer, the three slides from the Christmas stocking are lined up neatly.

He pushes a button, and a large rectangle of light materializes on the curtains. Inside it are some blurry, gray smudges that don't really look like anything, but then he grabs the edge of the lens, turns it—and suddenly the image becomes sharp.

Chloe crosses her legs and leans back on the couch. She is a bit surprised. She had expected to be able to see more details once it was magnified, but this is far sharper than she had imagined. What were indistinct shadows when she saw them on the small slide are now clearly visible. Trees, rock ledges, paths on the mountainside.

Not to mention the cabin itself. It's also much more detailed in this enlarged version of the photo. Having said that, though, it's still just that; a photo of a landscape with the cabin in the center. If, in fact, there is a clue to a Christmas treasure hunt hidden in it, she certainly isn't able to spot it.

A click, a sleepy, gliding sound, another click, and then the next image appears on the curtain. The slide from day two of the vacation. The third of December.

"It's just the same," Chloe sighs. Why it bothers her so much now, she doesn't quite know. After all, she came to the same conclusion the first time she saw it.

"Not completely," says Abby, who is sitting next to her on the couch. "The angle is different, so it's taken from another place. And ... there are tire tracks in front of the barn."

Chloe glances at her with squinted eyes.

"No, I'm serious," Abby insists. "Dad, go back to the other one for a sec, would you?"

"Sure."

Chloe tilts her head and stares at the curtains as he switches back and forth between the two images a few times.

Abby is not wrong. Chloe couldn't see it when she compared the miniature versions of the photos—in those, the driveway just looked white—but now she can make out the prints from a car's tires in the snow in one of the photos. Whether that information is in any way useful ... well, that's the question.

Up on the makeshift screen, the image with the tire tracks disappears, and the slide they found in the stocking this morning takes its place. Like the other two, this photo has the cabin in the center, but it's been shot from the opposite side so it shows the backyard.

And as it is magnified, a detail that neither of them had noticed before is revealed.

Chloe turns her face and exchanges a confused look with Abby, who opens and closes her mouth twice before finally looking up at their dad and saying:

"I ... don't get it. What does it mean?"

Even though it's him she's looking at, the answer comes from their mom, who sits in an armchair by the fireplace.

"It means that the photo was taken within the last few days," she says. "While we've been up here."

There's something in her voice that Chloe doesn't like. A tension that she herself also feels, even though she can't quite put her finger on why.

But the feeling *is* there—and it only gets stronger when Chloe's gaze slides back up on the curtains and locks onto the work of art she made with her older sister out in the backyard.

The Adorable Snowman.

December 5th

Adam

On their fourth morning in the cabin, Adam is up before everyone else—and also before the sun. This was a decision he made the night before when the girls' snowman appeared on the curtains, and he set no less than two alarms on his phone to make sure he'd wake up.

Because just like his wife, Adam wasn't thrilled at the sight of the snowman on the slide. Despite trying to tell himself that it doesn't have to mean anything and that it's probably just an innocent game, he doesn't like the idea of somebody taking pictures of them. Of somebody watching them. Therefore, he intends to check the Christmas stocking before letting the girls near it. Just to make sure.

The living room is cold this morning, colder than it has been the other days. He notices this as soon as he starts walking down the stairs.

It has also been snowing while they slept. A lot. Even though the sun hasn't risen yet, he can see it quite clearly on the other side of the living room window; a blue-white sea, illuminated by moonlight. It's a lot higher than yesterday. Over at the barn, it almost reaches all the way up to the door handle.

He puts on his coat, braces for the cold wind, and opens the door. In front of it lies another large pile of snow, so he has to push to open it up all the way.

Outside, it's completely silent, and for a moment he stays put while his gaze wanders over the glistening surface of the snow and from there up to the dark blue velvet of the firmament. The moon and the stars float up there, brighter than he has ever seen them. It must be the clean mountain air.

Slowly, he starts making his way through the snow to get to the barn. It's no easy task. In the worst places, it reaches almost all the way up to his hip, and he wonders if his car would've been able to make the trip if this had been their last day instead of the day after tomorrow.

As he reaches the barn door, he stops once more. His gaze doesn't stray this time, though. It stays on the Christmas stocking. Like the snow, it also reflects the moonlight because its surface is covered in tiny ice crystals.

For some reason, this makes it feel strangely intimidating to him. As if it belongs in a dream rather than the real world.

He pulls off one of his gloves and examines the outside of the stocking, The overnight frost has made the fabric stiff, but it still gives way when he squeezes it —and it doesn't feel as if there's a slide in it. In fact, it feels empty.

Maybe the snow was also too much for our Secret Santa, he thinks, feeling a touch of relief. After all, the stocking being empty would make his day a lot easier.

Nevertheless, he needs to be sure. Ergo, he slides his hand down into the stocking.

At first, there is nothing. Only the rugged, icy surface of the fabric. But then there is something. Not a slide. Something soft.

He closes his fingers around it, pulls up his hand, opens it ... and hears his own breathing stop.

"What the hell is this?" he mumbles—and then once more, a little louder: "What *the hell* is this?"

In the palm of Adam's trembling hand lies a pile of small, scruffy feathers in shades of brown and gray.

He has seen feathers in the exact same colors before.

The headless chicken.

"He still isn't answering?"

The question comes from Beth, who stands in the doorway, staring at Adam as he sits on the edge of the bed with the phone's receiver pressed against his ear.

"Does it look like he has answered?" he hisses, demonstratively holding the phone out toward her—as if it were a broken vase and she the cat that had knocked it off the table.

Beth widens her eyes but doesn't say anything. Or rather, she doesn't say anything with words. Nonetheless, her body language is pretty unambiguous; crossed arms, a raised eyebrow, one shoulder leaning against the doorframe. She is, in other words, waiting for him to apologize.

Not gonna happen. Perhaps it's unfair, but Adam needs to get his own frustration under control before he can even consider worrying about hers.

Because he is upset. And with good reason. Their vacation, which started off so well, is veering completely off track.

The slides were one thing, but the feathers crossed the line. Best-case scenario is that it's a joke, a distasteful prank. Worst case is ... what? It's so bizarre that he can't even come up with a real guess as to what the purpose could be.

Aside from scaring us.

If so, it has worked as intended. The first thing he did after the immediate shock of seeing the feathers was to tear the Christmas stocking down from the nail and throw it in the trash. The second was to march up here and call their holiday host to find out if he knows anything about it.

That was half an hour—and about twelve unanswered calls—ago.

That realization makes Adam take the receiver away from his ear and put it back on the phone base.

"We should never have come up here," Beth sighs in the doorway. "It was a bad idea."

What she's really saying is that it was *his* bad idea.

"We couldn't have known that any of this would happen," he replies.

"No, not the thing with the stocking, of course. But ... nah, forget it."

"But what?"

She takes a breath but then hesitates and shakes her head as if to say that it doesn't matter.

"But what, Beth?" he repeats, knowing that insisting will only lead to an argument. But a part of him also wants an argument. *Craves* it so that he can get an outlet for all the shit that is smoldering inside him.

"It's just ... I told you. I told you it was a bad idea to take the girls out of school in the middle of the semester, but you wouldn't let it go. We could have waited until the Christmas holidays, and then—"

"And then what? Exactly what difference would that have made? You think Secret Santa out there stays home during the Christmas holidays, or what?"

Instead of answering, Beth stares at him angrily and puts a finger over her lips ... and even though, deep down, he knows that she's right—that he ought to lower his voice for the sake of the girls—it only pisses him off even more.

"I insisted," he growls, "because I felt we needed to find each other again. Not just the two of us, but the whole family. All four of us."

"Well, if it keeps snowing, we'll probably have plenty of opportunity to do so," Beth mutters. "Who knows, maybe we'll end up spending the Christmas holidays here. Then maybe there will be slides under the tree."

"Oh yeah, that's just perfect! Blame me for the goddamn snow as well!"

Beth stares at him for a long time. Then she lets out a sigh of resignation and closes her eyes. When she opens them again, the anger has faded. In its place is a profound sadness.

"I think we should go home," she says.

"But we've only got two days left. We're supposed to go home the day after tomorrow anyway. And aside from that fucking stocking—which *has* been thrown out now, by the way—it's been good. I mean, the girls have had fun together, and the two of us have had a good time too, right?"

"Yeah, but ... I don't feel safe anymore, Adam. So maybe it's best to just throw in the towel and say that we gave it a fair shot."

Are we still talking about the trip, Beth?

"Listen," he says, his voice almost drained of its strength. "The stocking has been thrown out. It's *gone,* and even if it wasn't, the most likely explanation is still that it's just a really bad joke. So, could we maybe just take a breath and try to make the best of the last two days of our vacation? If we're lucky, some of the snow might melt over the next two days, so it'll be safer to drive."

For a long time—a *really* long time—Beth stands in the doorway, silent as the grave, her arms crossed, and her exhausted gaze fixed on him. Then she lets out a noise that lies somewhere between a sigh and a snort.

"What about the girls?" she says.

"What about them?"

"Do we tell them what was in the stocking this morning?"

Adam shakes his head.

"There *was* no stocking this morning, and there won't be one tomorrow either," he says. "The game is over."

Beth ponders for a moment, then nods, repeating his last words.

"The game is over."

December 6th

❦

Beth

To Beth's relief, Adam was right on both counts. Not only is there no Christmas stocking hanging on the barn door this morning, but a fair amount of the snow has also melted during the night. If it keeps thawing the rest of the day, the car should have no problem making the trip down the mountain tomorrow.

All in all, it's shaping up to be a good day. The girls have spent the entire morning together, and they haven't been at each other's throats at all. They've been playing chess on an old chessboard they found at the bottom of a cupboard, and about half an hour ago they went out to check on the animals and fix the snowman. Apparently, the thaw had cost him an arm and an eye.

Adam and Beth have also had a good morning, all things considered. Like her, he was a little tense when they got up, but after seeing that the nail on the barn door was empty, he lit up.

Right now, he is sitting in the armchair with his feet resting on the arm of the couch. Actually, that's also where Beth's feet are, because she's lying on the couch with a worn paperback edition of Randall Morgan's *The Flood* in her hands. Occasionally, their feet bump into each other by accident, and every time that happens, they exchange a glance and a smile.

Despite their recent ups and downs, she must admit that this is nice. Just being with him here in the cozy living room, listening to the crackling of the fire. No obligations and no distractions.

Whether it will have an impact on their relationship in the long run, as Adam is hoping for, only time can tell. But Beth doesn't want to waste her energy wondering about that now. Today, she just wants to relax and enjoy that the unpleasant mess with the Christmas stocking is over.

No sooner has she finished that thought than someone knocks on the window behind her. She jolts and jumps up, barely managing to catch her book before it falls to the floor.

It's Chloe out there. Her cheeks are red under the beanie, her eyes big. She's waving frantically with her mitten-clad hand to get her parents over to the window.

"What's the matter, Chloe?" Beth asks, feeling a tinge of panic when, instead of saying anything, her daughter shakes her head and holds up the mitten in front of her mouth.

"Why doesn't she answer?" Adam says.

Beth responds with a shrug and a nervous grimace as she scrambles over to the window—so quickly that she accidentally bumps one of her thighs against the armrest of the couch.

"What is it, sweetie?" she asks once she has gotten the window open.

Once again, the mitten moves up to Chloe's mouth. She shushes her mom and whispers:

"Hurry up and come out back, but don't make any noise."

Beth analyzes the voice as well as her daughter's face. Neither show signs that anything is wrong. She is whispering, sure, but she doesn't sound scared. Rather, excited.

"I'm not sure I understand, sweetie. What do you need us to do out there?"

"It's ... there's just something you need to see, okay?"

"So, nothing is wrong?"

"No, but you need to hurry. Otherwise, you're gonna miss it."

Beth looks over at Adam, who shrugs and then heads out into the hallway to put on his coat.

After a moment of hesitation—and an impatient *come on, Mom* wave from her daughter—Beth follows him.

Just as he rounds the east-facing corner of the cabin, Beth catches up to her husband, and like him, she comes to a complete halt after taking only one single step into the backyard.

Abby and Chloe are already back there, crouching next to the snowman. He isn't the one who has their attention at this moment, though. That honor belongs to the four living creatures walking among the trees on the other side of the fence surrounding the backyard.

A family of deer—a father, mother, and two fawns —moving with effortless grace across the snow-covered forest floor in small, ballet-like leaps. Occasionally, they pause to gently nibble on twigs and buds from the bushes along the backyard fence.

It's like watching a painting come alive, and Beth finds herself holding her breath as she studies the animals.

"Can we get closer?" Abby whispers.

"Maybe," Adam whispers back. "We're pretty far away from everything, so perhaps they're not scared of people."

With those words, he begins to approach the deer with cautious steps.

When he has reduced the distance between them and himself to about ten feet, something interesting happens. The animals don't flee, but they change their formation so that the largest, the head of the family, places itself as a clear barrier between Adam and its family.

It dawns on Beth that Adam is doing the same— walking in front of his family with his arms stretched out to his sides to protect them—and this realization triggers a sting of guilty conscience.

Because if she's being honest with herself, she hasn't been fair to Adam. She resisted when he suggested the vacation, and she has seized every opportunity to blame him whenever something went wrong—despite her knowing full well that he's doing it for their sake. For his family's sake.

There is no more than an arm's length between the two fathers now, and Adam slowly raises his hand, bringing it closer to the deer's nose.

The deer snorts, takes a step backward, and stays there for a moment with the gaze of its black eyes fixed on his outstretched hand.

And then—as nothing dangerous happens—it suddenly moves forward again and sniffs his hand.

Adam stays completely still and gives it time to examine him. Then he strokes it gently over its neck. This triggers another snort from the deer ... but it neither flees nor charges. It accepts his touch—and it also accepts the presence of the girls as Adam waves them closer.

The moment is magical, but it's also brief, because shortly after there is a shrill cry from a bird of prey somewhere up on the mountain, and this makes the entire deer family jolt and run off.

That's okay, though. Beth has no doubt that this will be a memory that the girls will forever cherish.

And she is grateful to Adam for giving it to them.

"Come on, Wigglebutt!"

"No, come on, Bumbleball!"

There is no lack of enthusiasm from the cheerleaders. The two competing athletes, on the other hand, could try a little harder, in Beth's opinion.

To be fair, they were given very short notice before being thrown into the sporting event, and they're unpaid ... at least if one doesn't count the lettuce leaves scattered around the corridors of the maze.

The game is called *Maze Chase*, and the concept is incredibly simple. It's a race. The goal is to be the first to get through the maze that Chloe and Abby have built on the barn floor using old boards, crates, garden tools, and other stuff that they've found lying around the place.

The athletes have been brought in directly from the rabbit cage; Bumbleball as Chloe's champion and Wigglebutt as Abby's.

So far, they're pretty even. Both are in the pondering phase, considering whether or not to round the first corner of the maze.

At least it's easy to tell the two apart. Wigglebutt is completely white, while Bumbleball, Chloe's favorite, is spotted and most of all looks like a soccer ball.

"Hey, that's cheating!" Chloe shouts as her older sister reaches down toward the bunnies.

"Oh, calm down. I was just going to help them around the corner. Both of them, okay?"

Chloe responds with a snort but still doesn't protest when Abby gives the rabbits a light push.

"Now, don't forget, it's just a game," Beth says.

"Yeah, yeah, Mom, we're just messing ... whoa, Wigglebutt is taking off!"

Beth looks down. Abby's right, the white ball of fur has indeed picked up the pace. It rounds one corner, then another, and ... is brought to a full stop by a lettuce leaf that's just a little too tempting.

This gives Bumbleball its big chance, and it doesn't let it go to waste. It lazily trots past its opponent and continues in the same manner through the rest of the maze. At one point, it hesitates next to a lettuce leaf, but unlike Wigglebutt, Bumbleball is content just sniffing it.

And therein lies the key to victory. Bumbleball crosses the finish line and sends Chloe into a euphoric dance of joy on the barn floor.

"It's just because you're spoiling Bumbleball and feeding her all the time," Abby says.

"You're just mad because you lost," Chloe replies.

Abby doesn't sound mad at all, though. She sounds like she's on the verge of bursting into laughter—and that makes Beth very happy. It's been a long time since she's seen the girls enjoying themselves together the way they have in the past few days.

"Do we have time for a rematch?" Abby asks.

Beth looks at her wristwatch and frowns.

"I'm afraid it's already past your bedtime. But we aren't leaving until tomorrow afternoon, so maybe you can do it tomorrow."

"But we've set it all up, and Dad moved the car out of the barn and everything. If we do it tomorrow, we'll have to build it all again."

Beth bites her lower lip and looks back and forth between the pleading puppy eyes of her daughters.

"How about we meet halfway?" she says. "I'll tell Dad to leave the car outside tonight so the maze can stay. But then I want you under the covers in ten minutes. Deal?"

"Deal!" the girls exclaim in unison.

"Good. Then hurry on in and get ready for bed. I'll put the cottontails back in the cage."

"Thanks, Mom," the girls answer, once again in chorus, after which they stroll out of the barn, arm in arm.

For a moment, Beth stays put, listening to them as they move across the driveway. They're laughing and giggling like a couple of schoolgirls. Like best friends.

As the sound dies down, Beth shifts her focus back to the maze, where both rabbits have now found a lettuce leaf to munch on. She lifts them up, one at a time, and carries them over to the cage. Afterward, she turns off the lights in the barn and steps outside.

Walking across the driveway's white blanket of snow, which glistens in the moonlight as if each snowflake contains its own little light, Beth lets her gaze wander across the landscape. At this time of day, it's a fascinating sight, with the mountainside divided into strongly contrasting areas of light and darkness. Where the moonlight touches, the snow lights up in a sharp, white color, and where the shadows fall, it's pitch black. In many ways, it resembles an oversized map with white islands in a huge black sea.

Just as this thought goes through her head, two faint glows of light appear in the black sea, as if there was a ship out there.

But it's not a ship. Beth knows because she has seen the same lights before.

And how can she be so sure? The colors. One light is red while the other is white.

The light comes from the vehicle she saw further up the mountain the other day. The snowmobile with the broken taillight. The one that hurried away when she spotted it.

No need to be dramatic, she says to herself. *It's far away. Besides, it's probably just a mountain ranger or something.*

Could be. Still, it doesn't change the fact that the cold out here suddenly feels overwhelming. As though, all of a sudden, the temperature has dropped several degrees.

And even though this day has been great in many ways, she feels relieved that they'll say goodbye to this place tomorrow.

December 7th

❧

Abby

No child likes to hear panic in their parents' voices, and Abigail Gray is no exception. So, when she wakes up to the sound of her mom's voice, shrill and full of distress, she opens her eyes and sits up in bed with a gasp.

"Adam, it's back!"

Those are the words her mom yells—and even though there are two walls and a hallway between the rooms, Abby hears them loud and clear. It also doesn't take her long to figure out what it is that's *back*.

Her theory is reinforced when she hears her dad curse and then stomp down the stairs—and as he rips open the front door downstairs, Abby jumps out of bed and runs to the window upstairs.

Yup. She was right. Her dad is heading for the barn, where the Christmas stocking has been hung up on the door again.

When he gets there, he pulls the stocking down

from the nail, looks inside it—and then he does a whole lot of things that make no sense to Abby.

First, he lets go of the stocking and lets it fall to the ground. It doesn't look like it's something he does on purpose, though. More like a reflex. As if it was scorching hot and he burned his fingers on it.

He does pick it up again, but not before glancing back over his shoulder, seemingly to make sure that no one is watching him. Clenching the stocking in his hand, he then walks over to the garbage container.

No, he doesn't *walk*. He *marches*. As though he is angry or upset.

Almost as a confirmation of this thought, he now swings his arm in an arc and flings the Christmas stocking into the container, after which he—aggressively—rearranges the garbage bags, thus moving the stocking further down to the bottom.

After slamming the container's lid way too hard, he walks back to the barn door. Abby's first assumption is that he intends to remove the nail so that the stocking can't be hung up again. To her surprise, though, it's the snow in front of the door that he is focusing on.

He kicks, scrapes, and stomps like a maniac until he is shrouded in a cloud of white. When he's done, he studies the result for a moment, then he opens the door and disappears into the barn. He's not in there very long before the door flies open again, and he comes marching out. This time in the direction of the cabin.

Abby's heart is pounding in her chest. She knows that it takes a lot to make her dad lose his temper. He is always the calm voice of reason in their home, yet what she just witnessed was anything but calm. It was a freaking tantrum. What the hell was in that stocking?

Downstairs, there's a slam from the door, followed by her parents' voices. She can't make out what they're saying, but there's no doubt that they're both upset.

She looks over at her little sister, who is lying in the other bed and has somehow managed to sleep through the entire show.

"Chloe? Hey, Chloe?"

No verbal answer, but she is moving under the covers. She is waking up.

Now, their parents' conversation is replaced by another sound, footsteps on the stairs. Shortly after, there are three short knocks on the door to the room.

"Girls, are you awake?"

"Yeah, Mom," Abby replies. "Or ... well, I am. Chloe is still asleep."

"Okay. Could you wake her up, please, and then we'd like you to start packing your things. We've decided to go home early."

"Okay, um ... why?"

A break. Then her mom clears her throat.

"The forecast says it's going to snow later, so we want to leave as soon as we can to avoid getting caught in it."

As far as improvised lies go, it's an okay performance. Abby might even have bought it if she couldn't hear the strain in her mom's voice. The fear in it.

"I'll make sure Chloe gets up," Abby replies, and after a short pause she adds, "and we'll hurry, Mom."

"Thanks, sweetie. I'll make you some breakfast in the meantime."

A little over an hour later, everything is packed in the trunk of the car, and Abby is standing in the driveway with her little sister while their parents lock up the cabin.

"Could you hide the key, girls?" their dad shouts, after which he—without waiting for an answer—throws a small bunch of keys over to Abby. "Bill said we could just leave them under the big potted plant behind the cabin."

Abby catching the keys is more luck than skill, and it's only because the keychain's pendant, a small leather dreamcatcher, wedges itself between two of her fingers by accident.

"What about the barn?" she asks. "Shouldn't we lock that up too?"

"I already did that," Adam says.

Abby opens her mouth but doesn't have time to say anything before Chloe cuts her off.

"But ... what about the animals? We get to say goodbye to them, right?"

Their parents look at each other, and Abby can almost physically see a shadow glide over both of their faces.

"I'm sorry, sweetie," their mom says. "We really need to get going so we don't get caught in the snow."

"But I'm ... no, that's not fair! I want to say goodbye to Bumbleball!"

Chloe's voice is shaky and full of confusion—which is no wonder. It has, in every way, been a chaotic and confusing morning.

For Abby, on the other hand, all the small pieces suddenly start to fall into place. They don't complete the full picture yet, but enough of it to give her a premonition. A very disturbing one.

She glances down at the keys in her hand and then up at the cabin ... but when she starts moving, it's not in that direction. Instead, she walks over to the car where her dad has just taken a seat in the driver's side.

Since the car has been left out in the driveway all night, the glass of the side window is coated with a thin layer of ice that creaks when she knocks on it.

"What was in it?" she asks as he opens the door ajar and meets her gaze.

He plays dumb, assuming an expression of complete bewilderment as if he hasn't got the faintest idea what she is talking about.

"What was in the stocking this morning?" she repeats, pointing up at the window in the gable. "I saw you."

It only takes a split second before it's up again, but she sees his barrier crumble. She sees the surprise and discomfort flicker on his face.

"Nothing," he says with an awkward smile. "It was just another slide. I threw it out because it's our last day here, and ... and because, frankly, it's not funny anymore."

Why he lies to her, she doesn't know, but *that* he does, she has no doubt.

"I don't believe you."

He hesitates, glances toward Chloe, then down at the steering wheel and finally back at Abby.

"When we get home," he says. "I'll tell you when we get home. But right now, I just want to get your sister in the car without too much fuss. And I would really appreciate your help with that."

"When we're home. Do you promise?"

"I promise."

Abby nods, turns away from the car, and starts walking over to Chloe and her mom. However, she doesn't get very far before the sound of her dad's voice stops her again.

"No! You've got to be kidding me!" is what he says. "I don't believe this shit!"

"What's wrong, Dad?"

"It's the car. It's completely dead. Fuck!"

"What did he say?" Abby hears her mom ask as soon as the bedroom door opens upstairs.

"He'll come and pick us up," her dad replies. "An hour, more or less. He's gonna bring a mechanic too if he can get ahold of him."

"Oh, thank God. What about the stocking and the, um ... the thing this morning? Did you ask him if he knew anything about it?"

While asking the question, their mom lowers her voice, but not enough, and on the couch down in the living room, Abby and Chloe exchange a worried look.

"No, it wasn't exactly at the top of my list," their dad replies. "The car seemed more important, you know? Besides, I'd rather talk to Bill about it face-to-face once he gets here."

"Yeah ... yeah, sure."

The concern in her mother's voice is evident. Still, she somehow manages to tuck it away during the short walk down to the living room, so by the time she reaches her daughters, she greets them with a reassuring smile.

"Good news, girls. Dad talked to Bill. He'll come and pick us up in an hour."

"Nice," Abby says, after which she glances over to Chloe, trying to get her to pretend that they didn't hear every word of the hushed conversation.

Chloe doesn't reveal that they listened in. What she says instead isn't much better, though.

"That means we have time to say goodbye to the animals, right?"

The smile vanishes from her mom's lips in an instant, and she makes a strained swallowing motion.

"Or we could do something else," Abby hastens to say. "I was actually going to ask you if we should try that old Monopoly game you found."

"But ... you said you didn't want to," Chloe says. "You said it was boring and that it always takes too long."

Yup. And it's probably also missing half of the pieces, Abby thinks. But what she says out loud is:

"I've changed my mind, okay? You wanna play it or not?"

Chloe stares at her in disbelief but ends up smiling and jumping off the couch. And as she sprints up the stairs to get the board game, their mom walks over to Abby and puts a hand on her shoulder.

"Thank you for that, sweetie."

Abby is tempted to answer that she could thank her by telling her what the heck was in the stocking this morning, but she settles for a nod.

"Coffee table or dining table?" Chloe asks as she returns, carrying the Monopoly game under her arm. She sounds cheerful, as if she has forgotten all about the animals. This has Abby feeling a little ashamed. After all, she knows how much Chloe loves playing Monopoly, and it wouldn't have been the world's biggest sacrifice if she had said yes to a game earlier just to make her happy. That's what a good big sister would have done.

"The dining table," she replies and gets up from the couch. "I'll need a lot of table space for all my hotels."

"Ha! Keep dreaming."

"Oh, I don't need to. But let's first check to see if all the pieces are there."

"They are," Chloe says with a wry smile. "I checked on the first day when we found the game."

The world's worst big sister.

Chloe is right. All the pieces are in the box. And Abby is right too. The game does take a long time. So long, in fact, that they're still not finished by the time their dad heads upstairs to call Bill again, because he still hasn't shown up ... even though he should have been there over an hour ago.

"Did you get ahold of him?" their mom asks when he comes down the stairs again, and he answers her with a shake of the head and a heavy sigh.

"Nope. I don't know what's taking him so long."

"Maybe he's waiting for the mechanic," their mom suggests.

"I guess, but ... two hours?"

"He'll show up," her mom insists. She doesn't sound very convinced, though.

Half an hour later, the Monopoly game finally ends, and an hour after that, Bill still hasn't appeared. Both these facts have put a damper on the mood in the cabin. Her parents are frustrated by Bill's absence, and

Chloe is cranky because she wasn't the one who won the game

"I think I'll head out into the backyard," Abby says. "I'm bored."

"As long as you stay close to the house," her dad mumbles in a voice revealing that the couch is close to overpowering him.

"I will. Do you want to come, Chloe?"

Chloe considers for a moment and then shakes her head. That suits Abby fine. She wouldn't mind some alone time.

Outside, it has started to snow again. Not large flakes like the ones the other day, but rather tiny specks that can hardly be seen with the naked eye.

It's those that make the memory pop up in the back of her mind. The way they dance randomly in the air like a semi-transparent cloud of dust. Just like the one that surrounded her dad this morning when he kicked up the snow in front of the barn door. What the heck was he doing? And was it just anger, or was there a purpose to it?

She glances toward the windows of the cabin. The rest of the family is still sitting in there, none of them looking her way.

She fights a brief inner battle against herself, after which she speeds up and jogs to the barn door.

The first few layers that she scrapes off the pile with the edge of her shoe don't make her any wiser ... but then she suddenly reaches it.

The level where the snow has sporadic patches of a smudged, pink color.

"What the hell," she mumbles as she scrapes on, harder now. "What is this?"

Somewhere on the edge of her consciousness she realizes it, but her brain spares her and lets the comprehension trickle forth gradually. Like water from a spring.

But it *is* coming to her, and it is cruel. Because she finds one—and only one—explanation.

It's blood that has discolored the snow. Blood that must have dripped down from the Christmas stocking.

In the wake of this insight, another follows, and she instinctively spins around and runs over to the garbage container.

With quivering hands, she pulls garbage bags aside until the Christmas stocking emerges. She grabs it, lifts it up, and looks inside.

This time, her brain doesn't spare her. The recognition and the nausea hit her at the same time. She lets go of the stocking, lets it fall, just like she saw her dad do, then she turns away from the container and falls to her knees.

She doesn't vomit, but the impulse is there. It tenses the muscles in her stomach and causes her to let out a series of spasmodic wheezes.

Now she lies there, on all four like an animal, staring at the snow in front of her face. Except that she doesn't see the snow. She sees the severed rabbit's foot that lay at the bottom of the Christmas stocking, stained with dried blood. It's burned into her retina.

It was Bumbleball's foot. The pattern of the fur told her right away. White with black spots. Like a soccer ball.

Someone has cut the foot off Chloe's favorite rabbit and left it in the Christmas stocking for them to find.

Oh God. What if Chloe had been the one who found it?

It's too much. Abby's body can't contain it. She starts sobbing and gasping for air.

"Oh no, sweetie. Why did you do that? I told you I'd tell you when we got home."

She lifts her head, looks back—and sees her father standing in the driveway. He, like everything else in her field of vision, is broken into prisms.

She opens her mouth, wants to say that she's sorry, but only starts sobbing even more.

He doesn't say anything either. He just steps closer until he's close enough to help her up and embrace her.

"I don't want to be here anymore, Dad," she mumbles into his chest. "Can't we just go home now?"

He sighs and hugs her tighter.

But he doesn't answer her question.

December 8th

Chloe

In one of the boards in the wooden ceiling above Chloe's bed is a knot that looks like a squinting eye. It stares at her, and she stares back. She has been doing that for over an hour.

What happened in the nightmare that woke her up, she can't remember anymore. It must have been bad, though, given that her pillow was damp with sweat and her bangs were sticking to her forehead.

It's night still, and the room's only light source is a dusty beam of moonlight shining in through the window. It's faint, only tracing the outline of the room's furniture as well as her older sister sleeping in the other bed.

Yet, the dark brown knot up there—the eye—she can see quite clearly for some reason, despite the darkness. An oval recess with a spherical pupil in the center.

For a moment, her imagination plants an idea in her head—that the eye might wink at her—and all of a sudden, this is the last place in the world she wants to be.

She also doesn't really understand why they chose to stay another day. Her mom and dad said that they have to because the car doesn't work and it's too dangerous to walk down the mountain on foot. That they have to wait for Bill.

But Bill didn't show up yesterday, and he didn't answer when they tried to call him. So maybe he won't come at all ... and then they'll have to walk, right?

Something else is bothering Chloe too. She has the sense that something is going on up here. Something that scares the others and that they don't want to tell her about. They think she doesn't know, but she can feel it. It has something to do with the Christmas stocking ... and it also has something to do with the barn, because she wasn't allowed to go in there all day yesterday.

That won't fly today, though. If they have to stay another day, she wants to know what is going on. Otherwise, she intends to figure it out on her own.

She turns to her side and closes her eyes, trying to force herself to fall asleep. It doesn't work. The river of thoughts only flows quicker in the darkness behind her eyelids. Besides, the new position makes her aware that she needs to pee.

She glances at the door and then toward her sleeping older sister.

Abby is gonna lose it if Chloe wakes her up now ... but the door looks big and intimidating in the moonlight. And behind it, the dark hallway awaits.

Pull yourself together. You're nine years old!

Yup, but that doesn't change the fact that her stomach tightens at the thought of having to cross the dark hallway to get to the bathroom.

Maybe she doesn't need to wake Abby per se. She could bump into something by 'accident,' and if the sound was loud enough for her to wake up, well ...

Don't be such a baby, she orders herself. *This is why they don't tell you anything.*

She puts on a determined facial expression, pushes off the comforter, and swings her legs over the edge of the bed. Then she gets up and tiptoes her way to the door.

It creaks as she opens it but not loud enough to wake Abby, which Chloe feels both relieved and disappointed about.

The hallway is covered in darkness, and even though the bathroom door at the end is only about twenty feet away, she can't see it. It has vanished into the shadows. In fact, it's so dark in that part of the hallway that she might as well walk with her eyes closed. She wouldn't be able to see if she bumped into anything.

Or anyone.

A horde of invisible ants crawls over her arms and her neck at the thought, and she has to fight the temptation to retreat back into their room to wake Abby.

She moves her gaze to the left, in the direction of the stairs. That's where the light switch is. At least that is still visible.

On the other hand, so is the stairwell. It looms like a gaping black hole right next to it—and it isn't hard to imagine that something could be hiding down there. Lurking.

It's her imagination, even in her present state of unease she is able to understand that, but she could swear that she heard a faint creaking of wood. As if someone slipped down the steps of the stairs at the very second that she had that thought.

A moment to gather the courage, then another— and then she takes three quick steps over to the switch and flips it.

The light pours in on her, transforming her world into a white, rolling sea. It hurts, forcing her to shield her eyes with both hands even though she doesn't want to block her view. She wants to know if something comes for her.

Nothing comes leaping, neither before nor after she lowers her hands. It's just her. She is completely alone in the narrow hallway, which—bathed in bright, white light—is no longer frightening.

Relieved, Chloe turns her back to the staircase and fixes her gaze on the bathroom door. She doesn't intend to waste another second on little girl nonsense. She's going to pee, and then she's going to sleep. Period.

That is the plan. Therefore, she keeps her eyes locked on the target and shuts off everything that could potentially spark her imagination again.

This includes the stream of cold air that is let into the cabin and finds its way up to her neck when someone opens and closes the front door downstairs.

Calling the atmosphere at the breakfast table *tense* wouldn't be unreasonable. In fact, it's verging on an understatement. All the members of the family sit quietly, staring down at their plates—and Abby completes the picture by drumming nervously on the edge of the table.

Chloe has seen her big sister do the same thing many times before. Usually, it's because Abby has broken a rule and is waiting for a scolding. Today, however, both her parents look just as insecure as her.

"What's going on?" Chloe suddenly exclaims, to her own surprise as much as to theirs. "Why didn't Bill show up, and why can't I go out to the barn?"

On the other side of the table, her parents look at each other. Then her dad sighs and nods.

"You're right," he says. "It's not fair to keep you in the dark. The truth is that we don't know what happened to Bill yesterday. I tried to call him all afternoon and evening, but he never picked up. I plan to make another attempt this morning, and if he still doesn't answer ... well, then we have to find another solution."

"You mean, we're going to walk down the mountain?"

Her father puts on what is probably meant to be a reassuring smile, but it doesn't come across as genuine. It feels forced. Like bad acting.

"Well, it hasn't quite come to that yet," he says. "What we can do, though, is to call 911. Get the police to come and pick us up. That's probably the best solution anyway. Bill's SUV is fine and all, but they'll likely have some more suitable vehicles. Because it doesn't look like the weather is going to let up anytime soon."

Chloe turns around on her chair and looks out the window. She hadn't noticed it, but he's right. The air is full of large snowflakes, and the driveway is once again buried under a thick layer of white.

"Well, if everyone's done, how about we get the table cleared?" their mom asks in a voice that's a little too eager, after which she hands her empty plate to Chloe. "Would you mind doing the dishes today, girls?"

It's a decent attempt, she has to give her that ... but Chloe isn't going to let herself be distracted that easily. She still needs an answer to her second question, and therefore she rejects her mom's plate with a shake of the head.

"Why is the barn still locked up? What is it I'm not supposed to see in there?"

The words are allowed to hang in the air for a few long seconds while both parents struggle to avoid her gaze. Then her dad clears his throat.

"It's Bumbleball," he says. "It's ... it's gone."

"It got out of the cage somehow," her mom hastens to say. "And we know how much you adored it, so we didn't want to say anything until we were absolutely sure."

Chloe looks at her older sister and swallows a lump that feels like a golf ball when Abby confirms the story with a nod.

She can't claim to be completely surprised, because she had the feeling that it had something to do with the animals. But still, she can't quite shake the feeling that they're only giving her part of the truth.

However, after a moment of consideration, she decides that she isn't going to pursue it further. Maybe —just maybe—it's because she peripherally registered that her mom used the past tense when saying that they knew what Bumbleball meant to Chloe.

How much she *adored* the rabbit.

"You know what?" her mom says as she reaches over the dining table again, using her free hand to pick up Chloe's plate. "I've changed my mind. I'll do the dishes. Then the three of you can head out to the barn and check on the animals. Adam, could you—"

"I'll check first," he interrupts and nods, after which

he leaves the table and heads out into the hallway. "You can get ready in the meantime, girls."

The girls do, and the timing is perfect, because just as they have tied the last bows on their winter boots, their dad returns from his trip to the barn. A journey that—despite the short distance—has filled his hair with half-dissolved snowflakes and colored his cheeks pink.

"How did it look?" their mom asks from inside the living room.

"Fine," he replies, breathing on his hands and rubbing them together. "The barn looks normal."

"And there still weren't any ... surprises on the door?"

"None."

It's the Christmas stocking they're talking about. Why they have to beat around the bush like that, Chloe doesn't understand. On the other hand, she has the feeling that sometimes they just speak in code out of habit from when she and Abby were little. So maybe that's just it.

"Ready?"

Chloe nods and steps outside—only to stop abruptly again.

The wind is merciless today. Even the thick woolen scarf, which she wears in two layers around her neck, must admit defeat. The freezing air whips right through the fabric.

"Stay behind me and Abby," her dad says. "Then we

take the worst of it. And turn your head so you don't get it directly in your face."

Chloe follows both pieces of advice. She moves in behind the other two and turns her face away from the wind.

And it's this small action that will come to turn the parents' unease this morning into outright panic.

For as she turns her head, her gaze moves down into the backyard, where it finds the snowman.

And the thing that has been tied around his neck.

In many ways, Chloe Gray is a privileged girl. She comes from a good home with loving parents and a sister who is always there for her when it matters. She has also been blessed with good friends and is generally doing well in school, both socially and academically.

These things don't mean that she hasn't experienced hardship and frustration in her life. Of course she has, as have most other kids her age.

But Chloe has never—*never*—experienced the feeling that permeates her body in this moment.

The desecration. The indignation. The insult.

Someone—a person she doesn't know, and who therefore by definition doesn't know her either—has vandalized their snowman.

His eyes are gone, two creepy holes left in their

place. His mouth is warped so that he almost looks like he's screaming. His arms, two curved twigs, are halfway broken and folded in across his chest. It looks like he's hugging himself. *Comforting* himself.

But the worst part is the noose. The wrongdoer has tied a loop around the poor snowman's neck with a piece of string, presumably to signal that he's about to be hanged.

"Who did this?" Chloe hears her sister ask in a shaky voice. She is obviously also shocked.

The question is addressed to their dad, who is standing right next to her, but he doesn't answer. He just looks at the snowman and then back at her with wide-open, confused eyes, as if he hasn't understood a word of what she said.

"Um ... Dad?" Chloe tries, but she doesn't get an answer either.

"Who did this?" Abby repeats, this time a little louder. "Is it the same ..."

She hesitates and casts a strangely shameful glance in Chloe's direction before finishing her question in a lowered voice.

"Is it the same guy? The one who did the thing with the stocking?"

"I DON'T KNOW! OKAY, ABBY?"

Their dad's outburst causes both girls to jolt in fear and take a step backward. That is yet another new feeling for Chloe. He has raised his voice before to get her to behave, but this is the first time that he has actually scared her by doing so.

"I'm sorry, girls," he says in a gentler tone, holding his hands up in front of him. "I shouldn't have shouted at you. This isn't your fault."

"It's okay, Dad," Abby says, but he continues anyway.

"It's just starting to get to me, you know? All of it. The car. The animals. Bill not showing up. The stocking. And now this."

As he says the last words, he gestures toward the snowman ... and then he suddenly freezes.

"What's wrong, Dad?"

"It's not a string," he mutters, after which he walks over to the snowman and runs a hand along the noose tied around its neck.

"Sorry, what?"

"It's not a string," he repeats, pushing past his daughters and running toward the cabin. "It's a cable. A fucking telephone cable!"

In rare cases, the so-called *emergency meetings* in the Gray family can be about something serious, such as reprimanding the girls for making a habit of throwing the dirty laundry on the floor rather than in the laundry basket. As a general rule, though, calling an emergency meeting means something fun, like coming up with ideas for activities on a summer vacation or choosing which movie to watch on a spontaneous trip to the cinema.

Today, however, there is no doubt about the gravity of the situation when Adam calls his daughters down to the living room and asks them to take a seat on the couch because they're having an emergency meeting. It's one thing that he sounds upset and frightened, but on top of that, two objects that Chloe immediately recognizes have been laid out on the coffee table, foreshadowing the topic of the meeting.

One of the objects is the severed piece of telephone cable, which was tied in a noose around the snowman's neck. The other is the Christmas stocking. Chloe hasn't seen the latter since their third morning up here when they found the slide with the picture of the snowman. However, there has clearly been something else in it since then. The bottom half is discolored and dark red as if it has been ... wet?

"Mom and I have talked about it," their dad starts. "And we agree that it's time for you to know what's going on."

"We're not trying to scare you," their mom adds. "But at the same time, it's getting so serious that we have to make sure that you're being careful. Does that make sense?"

Abby nods firmly, and so does Chloe ... although, frankly, she's more than just a little confused right now.

"We're not alone up here," their dad continues. "There is someone out there watching us and ... well, frankly, trying to frighten us."

He reaches down, picks up the telephone cable, and shows it to Chloe and Abby.

"This isn't just any cable. It's the cable from the cabin's landline phone. Someone has cut it and removed it. And without it, the phone is useless, so we're no longer able to call 911."

"Where was the cable?" Abby asks. "Before it was taken, I mean."

Their dad isn't eager to answer the question, that much is clear from his eyes, but he does it anyway.

"It was on the wall in our bedroom."

"So, you're saying someone was inside the house?"

"That's the only explanation we can think of, yes."

"When?"

"Impossible to say for sure, but probably last night."

"Jesus fucking Christ," Abby mumbles—and to Chloe's surprise, neither parent reacts to the swearing. That says a lot about the gravity of the situation.

"That's one thing," their dad says. "The other is this."

He picks up the Christmas stocking from the coffee table and stares at it while his face works its way through a palette of gloomy expressions.

"We haven't been completely honest with you," their mom says. "The stocking has been out there more mornings than just the first three. And there have been other things in it than just slides."

"Mom, I don't think we need to—" Abby begins, but their dad silences her by shaking his head and raising his hand.

"Mom and I discussed it, Abby," he says. "And it's time for all the cards to be laid on the table. For your own sake."

He takes a deep breath and then turns his gaze to Chloe, who suddenly feels very small.

"Bumbleball didn't run away, sweetie. It was taken from its cage, and we, um ... we found something in the Christmas stocking that leads us to think that it's not alive anymore."

She hears what he says, but she has trouble decoding the words. It's like staring into a kaleidoscope where the patterns are constantly changing, so it's impossible to hold on to an image. Only when she feels the gentle touch of Abby's hand on her back does it sink in properly.

"Bumbleball is d-dead?"

"I'm sorry, sweetie. This isn't how we planned to tell you, but with everything that has happened over the last few days, we can't keep pretending nothing is wrong. You need to understand just how serious this is so you'll stay vigilant. And so you understand why we need to follow a pretty strict set of rules from now on."

"What rules?" Abby asks.

"First of all, no walking around alone. Especially not outside. And yes, that goes for Mom and me too.

Secondly, you keep your eyes open—and if you see anything weird, you let us know. Even if you think it's probably nothing."

"But ... you make it sound like we're going to stay up here," Abby says. "Can't we just go down to the town?"

Their parents exchange a tormented look, and their dad shakes his head.

"Unfortunately, it's not that easy," he sighs. "Do you remember how long it took to get up the mountain? And that was by car. On foot, I'm not even sure we can do it in one day. Especially not with the amount of snow that's out there now. And even if we get down to the main road, we're still far from Crimson, which is the nearest town. That was the town where we met with Bill at the gas station when we—"

"I don't want to stay," Chloe exclaims, rubbing her tear-filled eyes with the bottom of her palms. "I want to go home!"

Her dad steps closer and crouches in front of her. Next, he strokes a hand over her shoulder.

"I know, sweetie. But we have to wait for some of the snow to thaw so it's less dangerous for us to walk. We'll just have to try to make the best of it, okay?"

"We've talked about putting your mattresses on the floor in our bedroom so the four of us can sleep together, just like we did when you were younger," her mom says. "That could be kind of fun, don't you think?"

Chloe nods and purses her lips in a frozen smile,

but it's pure acting. A role she takes on solely for the sake of her parents.

Because she knows that the real reason why they want the girls to sleep in their bedroom is completely different.

December 9th

Adam

"You know this isn't going to last, right?" Beth whispers in Adam's ear as the early light of dawn slowly creeps across the bedroom floor in front of the bed, closing in on the two sleeping girls lying on mattresses down there. "Snow or no snow, we can't stay up here. Not as long as that maniac is strolling around out there."

Adam rubs his face and nods solemnly. He has had the same thought, and he doesn't disagree. The problem is that it feels like stepping out on a tightrope and not knowing if there is a safety net stretched out over the ring down behind the blinding spotlights. To leave the cabin would mean giving up a number of important things. Things like water, food, and heat.

Particularly the latter two worry him. Because he isn't exactly the outdoorsy survivor type. The closest he gets to building a campfire is lighting a disposable grill in the backyard for the annual summer party at home.

And one year this resulted in a large, scorched patch of grass that his neighbors quickly dubbed *Adam's crop circle*—a recurring topic of conversation every year. So, he has his concerns about whether he'd be able to take care of his family if they were to get stuck out in the snow.

He lifts his head from the pillow and glances down at the girls. They're still sleeping like logs. Oh, how he wishes he could just tiptoe over and pick them up, carry them down to the car, and drive back home with them snoozing in the back seat, just as he used to do when they were little and a visit or a family party had drained all their energy. Heck, he wishes someone would pick *him* up while he was sleeping and take him home.

This is wishful thinking, of course, and neither he nor the girls are going to sleep their way out of this.

"Tomorrow," he whispers. "We'll prepare for the journey today, and then we'll leave tomorrow morning."

Beth stares at him with eyes that contain something he doesn't like. It's not exactly anger, but close. Disappointment, perhaps. In the end, however, she nods, after which she carefully pulls off her comforter and sits up in bed.

"Are you getting up already?"

"I'm going down to make breakfast. I ... need to think about something else. A break."

"Wait for me," Adam says. "I'll go with you."

"You don't have to."

"Actually, I do. It won't look very good if that's the first thing the girls see when they get up, will it? Us breaking our own rule about not walking around alone."

For a while, Beth sits still on the edge of the bed, her back turned to him so he can't read her face. Then she shrugs her shoulders in what he assumes is a *fair enough, then let's go* gesture, upon which she gets up, slips into her robe, and quietly leaves the bedroom.

Adam does the same, except that he puts on a sweater and a pair of jeans before following her downstairs.

He finds her standing in the middle of the living room, a hand on her neck and her eyes locked on the coffee table.

Damn it, Adam thinks. *So much for thinking about something else. Why didn't we pack away that crap last night?*

"I'll get it," he whispers, stroking Beth's arm as he passes her on the way to the coffee table. Once there, he picks up the Christmas stocking and the cable.

His plan is to throw both into the garbage container outside, but that solution is trumped when his gaze wanders to the left.

Hell yeah. Be done with it once and for all.

"You go ahead and get started on breakfast, honey," he says. "I'll take care of this in the meantime."

Beth looks at the Christmas stocking in his hand and then follows his gaze over to the wood-burning stove. And then, for the first time on this cold morning, she smiles at him.

If ever there was a perfect definition of the concept of *cleansing fire*, this has to be it: The flames behind the sooty glass door of the wood-burning stove, greedily eating away at the symbol of their distress in the last days. The Christmas stocking, whose bright red color gradually turns black while the threads of the fabric melt and char.

Adam could spend a good while just sitting here staring at it. In fact, he probably would have if it wasn't for the sound of creaking steps behind him.

"Good morning, girls."

"Good morning, Dad. What are you doing?"

"Lighting the stove. It was freezing down here."

"Did it snow again last night?"

"A little."

"So, we won't be going home today either?"

The disappointment in Abby's voice is so tangible that Adam can almost feel it as a physical weight on his shoulders.

"No, we're going to spend the day up here. But it *will* be the last one. Mom and I have agreed that we'll give it a day ... and if we still haven't heard anything from Bill, we'll go hiking tomorrow."

"Down the mountain?"

"Yup."

"Isn't it dangerous?"

Definitely. Some would call it insane.

"Well, we have the road we can follow. Of course, it will take some time, but if we get up early, we'll have the whole day for it."

Silence and skeptical eyes. That's the answer he gets from both his daughters. He can't blame them for that. If he's not even sure it's a good idea, how can he expect to sell it to them?

As the day progresses and he doesn't spot Bill's SUV, no matter how many times he looks down the road, it becomes increasingly clear to Adam that help won't come by itself. They will have to take matters into their own hands. Therefore, he starts preparing for tomorrow's hike as best he can. He chooses his warmest outfit and asks the others to do the same. Next, he gets Beth and Chloe to prepare a backpack for the trip with food and water, as well as a first aid kit they found in a cupboard in the bathroom, while he heads over to the barn with Abby to fill the feed troughs so the animals won't starve.

In truth, Adam also has another agenda in there. He intends to see if he can find a tool in the barn that he can use as a weapon in case they need to defend themselves. After all, they're going out into nature and risk encountering wild animals.

That's how he presented it to Beth earlier, even though they both know full well that it isn't bears or wolves that haunt the back of his mind. It's their stalker. Their Secret Santa, whose gifts are as disturbing as they are crude.

The assortment of potential weapons is gathered in the southwest corner of the barn, just to the left of the pigs' enclosure, and while Abby fetches feed for the chickens, Adam takes the opportunity to study them closely.

There are several good options—a hammer, an axe, a metal pipe—but his choice falls on the pitchfork that he has previously used to change straw on the floor inside the pigpen. It has an advantage over the other tools because he can use it as a walking stick on the trip. Meanwhile, its tines pose a solid threat to a potential opponent.

Are you hearing yourself? Since when was 'just in case' an acceptable excuse for trudging around with a fucking pitchfork?

Since a stranger cut the foot off their daughter's favorite rabbit and put it in a Christmas stocking for her to find. That's the answer, plain and simple.

"Am I supposed to do everything myself?"

The sound of Abby's voice makes him jolt—causing both of them to burst out laughing.

"No, of course not," he says, putting the pitchfork

back with the other tools. "I'm coming. How far are you?"

"Everything but the pigs. If you get the feed from the cabinet, then I'll change their water in the meantime. Use the blue bucket in the back. It's the biggest one."

"You've really gotten the hang of this, huh?"

Abby winks at him and makes a gesture with her hand in front of her forehead, mimicking pulling down the brim of an invisible cowboy hat. Then, in a thick Texan accent, she says:

"Ain't my first rodeo, you know."

He responds by shaping a revolver with the thumb and index finger of his right hand and sending a bullet of approval in her direction.

Ten minutes later, the chores are done, and father and daughter stand together outside, taking one last look into the semi-darkness of the barn, before Adam pushes the door shut and locks it.

The pitchfork is also outside. It's leaning against the wall next to the barn door. Adam placed it there not long ago.

Abby saw him do it—and she also sees him pick it up again now and bring it with him to the cabin.

But she neither asks questions nor comments on it.

December 10th

∐

Beth

It's half past eleven in the morning, and the world is cruel and blindingly white. Only an hour and a half have passed since they left the cabin and set out on the long hike, but Beth is already starting to feel the exhaustion in her body.

And the despair. Can't forget that. It sneaks in on her, slowly but surely.

There are several reasons for this. The first, and biggest, is the weather, which hasn't improved at all since yesterday. Quite the contrary, actually. The wind is blowing fiercely, and the icy air carries thousands of snowflakes that swirl around them, stinging like angry insects in all the places where their skin is exposed. Every inhalation burns in their lungs, and every exhalation is moaned out.

Another—and for Beth, more surprising—reason is the isolation. With the snow lying like a heavy blanket over the landscape and no sign of life for miles, it feels as if they could easily be the last four people on Earth.

They aren't, though. At least one more person is out there—and in that fact lies the third reason for Beth's increasing sense of despair. *He* is out there. Their stalker, who has been hiding in the shadows while playing his sick game. He's the one who has driven them out here ... and there is a tiny part of her that is afraid this may have been his intention all along.

She glances back over her shoulder and catches sight of her daughters. They're walking next to each other, both with squinted eyes and cheeks that are red from the cold. Their breath forms white clouds that dissolve in the wind as quickly as they appear.

"Are you okay back there?"

Even though she speaks loudly, her voice is almost drowned out by the wailing of the wind, and she opens her mouth to repeat the question when Abby responds by raising a thumb.

"We're fine, Mom. It's just cold."

"You let me know if we need to slow down, okay?"

"Sure."

The answer is short, and there is a hint of irritation in Abby's voice, but it's not something Beth takes personally. After all, shouting back and forth takes energy, and this is the fourth or fifth time she has offered to adjust the pace for the girls.

Almost as an extension of that thought, Adam, who

has kept his place in the front the entire trip, pulls back so that he ends up next to Beth and says:

"I think it's better to just leave them alone. They'll let us know if they need a rest."

"I know," Beth replies. "To be honest, I just wanted to let them know that we haven't forgotten about them."

Adam raises one eyebrow but then apparently decides that this isn't a conversation worth the energy it will cost either. Instead, he picks up the speed again and returns to the leading position.

He must be feeling it too. The fatigue. Not only has he walked as far as the others; he has also created the narrow trench in the snow that they walk in. And that's no small task. In some places, the snow reaches almost all the way up to his hips.

At least they haven't had too much trouble following the road, even if they can't really see it. They have the milestones (which out here consist of old wooden poles painted orange at the top) to navigate by, as well as the pine trees adjacent to the road on both sides. However, Beth is pretty sure that there weren't trees lining the entire route when they drove up here. So, it might get harder soon. But they'll have to cross that bridge when they—

Her stream of thought is interrupted as she walks straight into her husband's back.

"Why are you stopping?"

Adam responds by raising his hand and pointing.

She follows the invisible line from his fingertip and feels her pulse increase slightly as her gaze finds what he wants to show her. A vehicle, parked in the middle of the road a bit further down the mountain.

A vehicle that she—despite the snow on the roof and the hood—instantly recognizes.

Bill's SUV.

It *is* Bill's SUV. That much is clear. But aside from that, more questions are raised than answered as the Gray family approaches the abandoned vehicle. Because several of the details Beth registers contradict each other.

One example is the amount of snow *on* the SUV and *around* it. On the roof and the hood there is snow, but it's a thin layer. As if it has been scraped off a short time ago. This would suggest that it was left here recently ... but then there's the road around the car. It's covered in snow, a layer as thick as what they've been walking through all morning, and there are no visible tire tracks behind it either. Ergo, it must have been parked here for a while. At least a day. Maybe two.

Another mystery is the door on the passenger side. It's open—and what possible reason could Bill have to leave it like that? The only explanation that even remotely makes sense in Beth's head is that something forced him to leave the car in a hurry. To run.

The problem with that explanation is that there are no footprints in front of the door either. There is some kind of track, but it's wide and uneven. It looks as though someone has dragged a bundle of branches across the ground in random patterns with no other purpose than to disturb the surface of the snow.

"I don't like this," Beth whispers as she and Adam approach the open door.

"Me neither," he replies, after which he looks past her and says, slightly louder, "You just stay there, okay, girls?"

"You said that already, Dad."

Adam exchanges a glance with Beth and shrugs. Next, he tightens his grip on the pitchfork he has been using as a walking stick and shifts his focus back to the task at hand. The abandoned vehicle.

"Do you see anything?" Chloe asks.

"Not yet," Beth replies. "The windshield is completely frozen, so we have to—"

Her voice disappears so abruptly that you would think someone had closed their hands around her neck and squeezed tightly.

That's also how it feels.

Behind the thin, semi-transparent layer of ice on the inside of the windshield is a silhouette, the shape and color of which are impossible to mistake once she has recognized them.

But ... he burned it! Adam burned it!

The idea is ridiculous, on the verge of downright

insane, because there are plenty of red Christmas stockings in the world, and of course, this isn't the same one.

Adam has spotted it now too. The color on his face tells her. He's as chalky white as the desolate snowy landscape surrounding them.

"Adam, don't," she tries to say as he pulls the car door the rest of the way open and reaches his free arm into the cabin, but her warning comes out as nothing more than a hoarse whisper.

The stocking hangs from the rearview mirror, and she can hear the string snap as Adam grabs it and pulls. It sounds like a whiplash to her ears.

When he has gotten the stocking out, Adam raises up the pitchfork in his other hand and jams its pointed end into a snow pile on the side of the road, leaving it to stand there on its own like a makeshift milestone. Next, he grabs the sides of the top edge of the stocking with both hands and opens it.

Even before seeing it with her own eyes, Beth knows it's something horrible, because she's never seen Adam's face so contorted in terror.

She holds out her hands, but he doesn't give her the stocking. He just stares at her with skeptical eyes. As if he wants to make sure she realizes there's no going back once she's looked inside it.

And when Beth finally runs out of patience and tears it out of his hands, she immediately learns that he's right. There is no turning back.

Smeared across the fabric on the inside of the stocking are thick, shiny stains of frozen blood. At the bottom is a severed finger.

"It's B-Bill," Adam stammers. "Oh God, Beth. It's Bill's finger."

"You don't know that," Beth replies in a voice that, for some reason, is deeply accusatory. "You can't know that!"

"But I do," Adam says, pointing. "It's his ring. It's got a dreamcatcher engraved on it. Just like the one in his car. It was because of his wife. He told me. She was ..."

He says something more—a whole lot, actually, because Adam is one of those people who can't stop blabbering when they're in shock—but Beth has stopped listening.

Because she has just spotted the next tidal wave in their endless sea of hardships.

The man is standing on a rocky ledge jutting out over the road further down the mountain. And he's holding something. Something long and black, which he now raises to eye level and aims at them.

It happens at the exact same moment. Beth realizing that it's a rifle—and the bang shattering the silence, echoing across the bleak, snowy landscape.

Beth sees it happen. She sees the shaft of the pitchfork split in half and break as the bullet pierces the wood with a force that is almost unfathomable. She sees splinters fly out in all directions before landing in random places in the pile of snow that Adam had planted the pitchfork in.

She sees it in eerie detail. For the same reason, she's also the first to understand what is happening—and that her actions in the next few seconds might mean the difference between life and death for her family.

"THE TREES!" she roars, while giving Adam a hard push to wake him from the state of shock he's in. Next, she runs toward her daughters. "THE TREES, ABBY! GET CHLOE INTO THE WOODS!"

Abby snaps out of the shock faster than her dad. She nods frantically, then grabs Chloe by the coat and pulls her toward the pine trees.

Beth glances back just in time to see Adam stumble and fall, but he immediately gestures for her to keep going.

Beth does. She ploughs through knee-high snow, groaning and snarling, to catch up to her girls, who have now been reduced to two colorful winter coats emerging sporadically among the tree trunks.

The next shot is going to come soon. He's had plenty of time to load the rifle, hasn't he?

The thought gives her the chills, and she has to concentrate to suppress the temptation to slow down and look back in the man's direction.

Only when she has gone further into the forest and

found shelter behind a wide tree trunk does she dare to glance behind.

Adam is right on her heels now. He is running in an uneven pattern, no doubt trying to make himself a harder target. Whether it will make any real difference if their pursuer should decide to send another bullet in their direction, however, Beth isn't sure.

Because she no longer believes it was a coincidence that he hit the pitchfork's shaft. She thinks it was deliberate, to scare them—which would also explain why he only shot the one time.

It's part of his game.

"The girls?" Adam moans as he catches up to her. "Where are the girls?"

Beth looks in the direction where she caught a glimpse of their coats between the trees a moment ago and feels a twinge of panic when she can't see them. Then she discovers something small and triangular in a dark purple color sticking out at the foot of a tree trunk a little further ahead.

Chloe's coat.

She points—and then uses all her energy to keep up as Adam runs toward them.

They find the girls sitting behind the tree trunk, huddled and clasping each other's hands. It's a heartbreaking sight, almost too much for Beth to handle. Had it not been for Adam grabbing her arm and giving her a stern look, her despair could very well have overpowered her.

"I know you're scared, girls," Adam says with a calmness that Beth honestly doesn't know where he finds. "We are too. But we can't stay here, okay? We need to get away from the road. That's the most important thing right now. As far away from it as possible."

The girls lift their heads and stare at him. Both look like they have thousands of questions swirling around behind their tear-filled eyes, but neither asks a single one. They're dead silent.

Adam doesn't speak either. He simply reaches his hands out and lets them hang in the air in front of the girls until they're ready to take them.

Now, they run together further into the snow-covered pine forest, hiding among shadows and tree trunks, while the road—their only sure guide to finding their way down the mountain—gradually gets smaller and smaller, until it finally disappears from sight.

It's a nightmare. Dusk is creeping in, the temperature is dropping alarmingly fast, and for Beth, it's no longer just a looming concern that they might be forced to spend the night out here.

It's an indisputable fact.

They're still in a wooded area and still on a mountain, though not necessarily the one they started on. That is the extent of her knowledge—and she has the feeling that the same goes for Adam, even though he tries to maintain the illusion that he hasn't lost his bearings and is still able to lead them down from the mountain.

Nevertheless, it won't be long before he also throws in the towel. She can sense it from his posture. The way he drags himself along, hardly lifting his eyes from the white blanket of snow on the forest floor.

To be fair, this is also where Beth's gaze is most of the time. But that's just because her fatigued brain keeps insisting that the naked branches occasionally sticking up from the snow are in fact hands with bony fingers that won't hesitate to grab their feet if given the chance.

And it's only a short leap from that thought to the image of Bill's severed finger at the bottom of the Christmas stocking flashing across her mind once more.

The girls are also on the brink of total exhaustion. They stagger along like two mindless zombies behind their parents, and neither has said a word for more than an hour.

"We're going to have to spend the night out here," Adam says, his voice hoarse and weak. "I think our best chance of a fairly dry spot is under the rock over there."

He points and Beth looks, but for a moment she is unable to see past the trees standing like ghostly pillars in the dim light. Then she spots it; a grayish-white out-crop protruding from an otherwise steep mountain wall, thus forming a natural canopy about ten feet above the ground. And Adam is right; there is a bare spot under the rock, which means that they'll be shielded from the worst if the night should offer more snow. Unless, of course, the wind changes.

Beth accepts his suggestion with a nod, and Adam turns to Chloe and Abby.

"Did you hear that, girls? Unfortunately, we'll have to sleep out here. I know it's not—"

"Okay."

One single word. That's all. No protests, no complaints, no questions. Just *okay*. Never has a single word from Abby hit Beth so hard.

Once they've reached the spot under the rock, Beth opens her backpack and pulls out a wool blanket along with some of the sandwiches she made with Chloe yesterday. She spreads the blanket on the dry—but still frozen—patch of forest floor beneath the rock before breaking the sandwiches in halves and handing them out.

She has more in her bag, but her common sense tells her they should start rationing. Just to be on the safe side.

Following the humble meal, the four members of the Gray family lie down on the blanket, the adults on the sides and the girls in the middle. There they lie, huddled together like matches in a matchbox, whispering words of comfort to each other while darkness gradually devours the snow-covered pines around them.

December 11th

Abby

Abby is only fifteen years old, but when she opens her eyes after spending the night on the frozen forest floor, she feels ancient.

Everything hurts. Her joints are stiff, her bones feel like they've been coated in ice, and any kind of activity —physical as well as cognitive—feels draining and painful.

Carefully, so she doesn't wake Chloe, who is lying against her left arm, she gets up into a sitting position. On the other side of her little sister, her mom is still sleeping, but the spot to Abby's right is empty.

Her dad, who was lying there, is now walking among the trees in the part of the forest that surrounds their camp under the rocky outcropping. His arms are full of branches of varying sizes.

Now, almost as if he has sensed her gaze, he lifts his head and looks in her direction. He doesn't say anything, probably to avoid waking up the others, but instead frees one hand from the stack and waves at her.

He looks marginally better than last night but is still just a shadow of his usual self. Pale, sunken, and exhausted.

In his defense, the same likely goes for her. Certainly, yesterday's trip and the excruciating night on the frozen ground have also left their mark on Chloe and their mom. Both look completely off. Their lips are blue, and the skin on their faces seems strangely ... polished? Almost wax-like.

Another agonizing effort gets Abby on her feet—and after massaging her calf muscles to bring them back to life, she walks over to her dad.

"Morning, Abby. Did you sleep okay?"

Is that supposed to be a joke? She honestly can't tell, so she decides to ignore the question and ask another instead.

"What are you doing?"

He looks down at the branches in his arms, then shrugs his shoulders and sighs.

"I'm gathering wood. For a fire, you know? But ... heck, I'm not even sure if I can get it going. Just figured I had to give it a shot."

Abby nods and smiles, but on the inside she's a bit shaken. She doesn't like how beaten he sounds. How self-condemning he sounds.

"Are the others awake?"

Abby shakes her head.

"No, they're still sleeping. Do you want me to help you carry?"

"No, it's okay, thanks. But you can get the lighter if you want to help. It's in the first aid kit at the bottom of the bag. I put it in there so it wouldn't get wet. While you're at it, you can also check the phones one more time. There was still no signal when I got up, but you never know."

Abby nods and, without hesitation, gets to work while he carries the firewood over to the campsite.

As expected, the phones are a disappointment. There isn't a trace of cell service. On the bright side, though, the lighter turns on at the first try—and the flame lingers. That was *not* the case last night when they tried to use it to warm their hands. The wind was stronger then, and they were lucky if they got a few seconds of heat from it before it went out.

Now, however, the wind has died down, and Abby allows herself to let the flame burn for a moment while she holds one hand over it. The heat stings and tingles in her frozen fingers; so painful and yet so wonderful at the same time.

With the lighter in her hand, she walks over to her dad, who is squatting while arranging the small branches and twigs in a pyramid shape. His movements are slow and determined, even though his hands are trembling with cold, and each branch is placed with care as if it's the most important thing in the world right now.

She hands him the lighter. As he takes it, she notices that his fingers are almost blue from the cold, and she bites her lip, suddenly very aware of how important it is to get a fire going.

He flips open the lid of the lighter, spins the wheel a few times, and sparks flicker in the dim morning light, but there is no flame—and Abby feels her heart starting to beat faster in her chest.

Is it her fault? Did she use the last fuel that was in the lighter when she warmed her hand a second ago? Has she just sentenced her family to freeze to death just because she—

A short, hissing sound and then a small flame finally emerges from the lighter. Above it, she catches sight of her dad's eyes, red, wet, and more focused than she has ever seen them before.

Carefully, he moves the lighter closer to one of the dry twigs, and Abby holds her breath. The flame plays hard to get, leaning away from the twig a few times, before at last giving in and grabbing hold of it. Shortly after, a thin pillar of smoke rises into the air.

"You did it, Dad."

He nods, lets out a heavy sigh, and then nods again.

A movement behind her makes Abby turn her head. It's her mother and Chloe, both now sitting up, staring at the fire with eyes full of sleepy confusion.

"You ... made a fire?"

Part of the syrupy timbre in her mom's voice must

be due to her just having woken up, but Abby has a feeling that this isn't the primary cause.

"Yup," her dad replies, nodding toward Abby. "Abby helped me."

"I got the lighter from the bag," she says. "He couldn't have done it without me."

Her dad winks at his wife, then leans forward and blows gently on the kindling, making his face light up in a warm, golden glow, while the world's most wonderful sound—the soft crackle of the fire—fills the air.

And for a moment, it feels as if everything is going to be fine. As if they'll be okay as long as they can sit here together and get warm.

That moment lasts about thirty seconds. Then another sound fills the air. It's coming from far away, but it's getting closer, and it's unmistakable. It's the sound of a motorized vehicle.

Probably a snowmobile.

"Damn it, Adam! That's not what I'm saying, and you know it. I'm just pointing out that there is a better chance of getting help if we go *down* the mountain instead of *up*."

"And I'm saying we won't find much help if that ... if *he* catches up with us before we reach the road. And we're not exactly hard to find, dragging a big, fat trail of footprints behind us, are we?"

"Would you please stop fighting?"

"And if one of the girls slips and falls down? Breaks a leg. What then?"

"Oh, give it a rest, Beth. We're talking about ... what? Twenty-five feet? Thirty? Not exactly Everest, now, is it? Besides, we'll be careful. I'll climb first and find the best route."

"Huh? Just like you found the best route for us yesterday?"

"Oh, okay. Throw that in my face. Did it feel good?"

"Won't you please stop fighting?"

"At least it felt better than sleeping on the ground last night. I'll tell you that much."

"Oh, and you think I enjoyed that, Beth? I'm doing what I can, okay? I'm sorry that I'm not a—"

"STOP FIGHTING, DAMN IT!"

Chloe's shrill outburst works. It silences both parents and shifts their gaze from each other's faces to their youngest daughter. There they remain while the echo of Chloe's words reverberates through the forest.

"Chloe is right," Abby says. "It's hard enough to be out here without you yelling at each other."

She pauses, preparing herself to be reprimanded by one or both parents, but neither of them says anything. They just stare at her.

"I, um ... I agree with Dad," she continues. "I think it

174

makes sense to make a false trail down here and climb up the rock."

Truth be told, Abby isn't entirely thrilled with the prospect of climbing. Heights in general. But she is even less enthusiastic about getting an unexpected visit from the man with the rifle. And he's still out there. She has heard the snowmobile, not just once, but several times during the day. It's as if he is deliberately revving the engine once in a while so they don't forget about him. Psycho.

"And what about you, Chloe? Would you prefer to climb too?"

"Well, um ... yeah, I guess I would."

"Well, then the majority has spoken," her mom says bitterly, gesturing up against the rock wall. "Have at it, Tarzan."

"We need to make the false trail first," her dad replies, after which he turns to the girls. "Abby, if you run left with Mom, Chloe and I will run right. Just head a bit into the woods and then turn around, okay? Not too far. And remember to stomp and kick so the track gets as messy as possible."

He keeps looking at the girls until he has received a nod from both of them. Then he turns to his wife. She also nods, albeit somewhat more reluctantly.

"Good, then start running."

That is, Abby quickly realizes, a very powerful word to use about what they're actually doing. They're not exactly running. *Stumbling* would probably have been a more apt description. There is no lack of effort, though —and the result is also quite satisfactory. They manage to leave a wide track in both directions. She even makes sure to run in figure eight patterns around a bunch of trees in the forest just as an added bonus. If nothing else, it ought to confuse their stalker a bit.

When Abby and her mom return to their starting point, her dad is already preparing for the climb. He is standing with one foot resting on a small notch a couple of feet above the ground, sliding his hands back and forth across the jagged surface of the rock wall to find the best grip. Luckily, there are plenty to choose from.

"Okay," he says, grabbing a hold and pulling himself up. "I think I've got it. Chloe, you wait until I'm three feet above your head, and then you follow. Abby, you do the same; wait and follow Chloe. And you go last, Beth. And all of you, take off your gloves so you get a better grip, okay? Any questions?"

"No, I think we got it," their mom says. "Just ... be careful, okay?"

"I will."

It's not just empty words. Even though he must be just as exhausted as the others, he takes the time to double-check every grip. And he also makes sure that the others have taken note of every single step in his route so they can copy it afterward.

The rock wall isn't as slippery as Abby had feared, but it *is* cold. So much so that her bare fingers are almost completely numb when she reaches the halfway mark.

Just don't think about it, she tells herself ... but of course, this has the complete opposite effect. Now, she can't help but stare at her fingers every time they close around a grip, wondering if they're strong enough to hold on.

Chloe, on the other hand, does surprisingly well. Several times she actually has to stop and wait to avoid bumping into their dad. When did she become such a little monkey?

"Are you okay, sweetie?" sounds from underneath Abby, and when she looks down, she is greeted by her mom's worried face.

"Yeah, I'm ... I'm okay."

"Are you sure? Your hands are shaking."

"They're just cold. I'm freezing."

Her mom narrows her eyes but says nothing.

"Did you fall asleep down there or what?"

Abby looks up and sees Chloe hanging sideways, one shoulder resting on a small outcrop. Not only is she almost at the top now, but the little punk looks relaxed too. As if this is the easiest thing in the world.

"Yeah, yeah, whatever, Chloe," Abby snaps. "We're coming."

"Be careful," her mom says, but Abby flat out ignores her. She's got something to prove now.

With clenched teeth, she finds the next grip and pulls upward. Then the next. Hand, foot, hand, foot. It's going fine. Her hands are trembling, and her vision blurs a little, but it's only a problem if she focuses on it. And she doesn't. Her focus is solely on the treads of Chloe's boots. To get up there before her little sister reaches the—

A sound—so low that she's barely able to perceive it—reaches her ears. It's a scraping noise, like when you drag a knife blade sideways across a cutting board to push slices of vegetables aside. It comes from within the part of the rock her left hand is clasping.

That's all she manages to register before it breaks off and she loses her balance.

A moment of dizzying weightlessness behind closed eyelids, then comes the counter-pull—as well as a terrible, crunching sound in her shoulder—as the hand that still has a grip on the rock wall breaks her fall.

The pain is immediate. It hits her shoulder like a freight train, a jet plane, a fucking meteor, and she screams.

Is she still holding on, or is her back going to collide with the ground in a second? She has no idea. Her whole world has been reduced to an area the size of a tennis ball. A small, flaming supernova inside her shoulder.

"STOP RESISTING, ABBY! I CAN'T KEEP HOLD-ING YOU! GRAB HOLD OF IT!"

She opens her eyes and sees her own hand being

led by another. It's her mom. She has grabbed Abby's wrist and moved her left hand over to a new grip.

"ABBY!"

The sound of her dad's voice, sharper than ever, serves as an ignition spark, causing Abby's fingers to close automatically around the grip. It also makes her look up ... but it's not him that her gaze meets. It's Chloe, her little monkey of a sister, who has now placed one of her legs in a crack in the rock wall so she can use her hands to hold on to Abby's coat.

"You need to use the other hand too, Abby," her dad says, now with his normal voice. "You need to climb."

"I ... can't. My shoulder, it ... I think it's dislocated."

"Shit. Can you stay there while I crawl down to you if Mom and Chloe help press you up against the wall?"

Abby closes her eyes, draws in air through her nostrils, and lets it out again in a strained sigh. Then she nods.

He hurries, and it probably doesn't take more than half a minute for him to get down to her. For Abby, however, it feels like a painful eternity, and when she feels his arm around her waist, she can't hold the tears back any longer.

"I know, sweetie," he whispers. "But I've got you now, okay? I've got you."

With his support, and with assistance from Chloe and her mom, Abby slowly pulls herself up the rock wall. Inch by inch, sting by sting, until they reach the top edge.

Getting past it proves to be the biggest challenge for Abby, as she doesn't have sufficient strength in her good arm to pull herself up. Consequently, her dad has to climb up first and pull her over the edge ... thereby bringing her shoulder into direct contact with the hard, uneven surface of the rock.

Once she is safely up, her dad lets go of her and starts helping the others while Abby lies on her back with her gaze fixed on the sky above. Her eyes are still wet, which causes the clouds to blur.

She blinks a few times to focus—and suddenly, it's no longer the clouds she's staring at. It's the faces of her parents. They look worried.

"I'm really sorry, Abby," her dad says. "But I have to try to move your arm to see if the shoulder is dislocated. It may hurt a little, okay?"

Abby shakes her head from side to side, but it's more in panic than protest, since she knows he's right.

"I dislocated my shoulder once," he says as he strokes a hand over her forehead. "Did I ever tell you that?"

"The trampoline on the basketball court," she replies and nods. "In high school. You said it hurt like hell when the doctors put it back in place."

"I was exaggerating to sound cool. But let's not jump to conclusions. After all, yours may not even be dislocated. I'll hold here, and when I tell you to, you push your arm upward, okay?"

"O-okay."

"Good, then give it a go."

Abby takes one, two, three deep breaths before clenching her teeth and pushing her arm upward.

It feels as if someone has drilled a knife into her shoulder and is now slowly twisting it around while she gasps and grinds her teeth.

"That's good," her dad says, his voice calm but firm. "You're doing fine. Just a bit more."

As he speaks, he turns her arm slightly, and suddenly Abby feels a sense of relief, as if something is loosening.

"It's not dislocated," he says, looking at her mom with tears in his eyes. "Could be a slight sprain, but as long as she can push like that, the shoulder is where it's supposed to be."

Abby meets his gaze and asks him without words if he's sure—and when he answers with a nod, she closes her eyes and leans her head backward so that it comes to rest on the snow.

Part of her wishes she could just stay right there.

A few hours later, the involuntary hikers find themselves on a snowy slope further down what—judging by the sun's position in the sky—must be the southwest side of the mountain. They're looking for a good place to spend the night.

Because they will be spending yet another night

out here. Abby made sure of that. It already cost them extra time to take the detour over the cliff to hide their tracks, and with her mishap on the wall, they were delayed further. And why? Because she didn't want to be outdone by her little sister. What a joke.

Chloe is—rightfully—also angry with her. She's been walking with her eyes fixed on the ground a few yards ahead ever since their dad examined Abby's shoulder. And during that time, Abby has been preparing her apology. She just needs to gather the courage to catch up to Chloe and deliver it.

The world's worst big sister strikes again. Not a bad title for a book on their relationship. She would clap at her own ingenuity ... if her right arm didn't hurt like hell.

Her mom isn't exactly in the best mood either. Surprisingly, she hasn't yet taken the opportunity to give their dad an *I told you so.* Maybe she reasons that his guilty conscience is punishment enough. On the other hand, she could just be saving it for the moment when it will hit the hardest.

Now her dad stops and looks down toward a small clearing at the end of the slope. It's surrounded by tall pines that pour in over it, almost forming a roof that can give them a bit of shelter.

"It's not as good as what we had yesterday," he says, pointing. "But I think it's the best we'll get here. So, unless you have a better idea ...?"

Certain that this must be the moment for the snide comment, Abby looks at her mom, but she doesn't say anything. Not even an *I HAD a better idea*. Her mom just nods and starts walking in the direction of the clearing.

Immediately after, her dad follows suit, but Chloe stays put—and Abby decides it's time to give her the apology.

"Hey, um ... Chloe?" she says, grabbing her sister's elbow. "Can I talk to you for a second?"

Chloe nods but doesn't lift her head and meet her gaze.

"It's, um ... about what happened when we climbed. I'd like to—"

"I'm so sorry," Chloe suddenly says. "It was my fault."

"You're ... what? How was it *your* fault?"

"I knew you'd try to climb faster when I teased you, and I did it anyway. But I didn't think that you w-would ..."

The remaining words dissolve into sobs and sniffles, and Chloe buries her face in her mittens.

"No, no, Chloe," Abby says. "It wasn't your fault. I wanted to apologize to *you*."

A break. Then Chloe slowly lowers her mittens, exposing her wet, confused eyes.

"You did? Why?"

"Because I was the one who acted like a jerk just because you were better than me at climbing. And because ... because it's my fault that we have to sleep out here again."

She lifts her good arm, puts it around Chloe's shoulders, and pulls her closer.

"Heck, sis. Did you really think I was mad at you?"

The answer is impossible to understand since Chloe has her face pressed into Abby's coat. Nevertheless, the message is clear.

"Are you okay, girls?" sounds from further down the slope.

"We're okay," Abby confirms. She looks down, meets Chloe's gaze, and whispers, "We *are* okay, aren't we?"

Chloe wipes her eyes with her sleeve and moves her head up and down.

"That's right," Abby says. "So now we just need to get through the last night on this crappy mountain, and then we'll be ready to go home tomorrow."

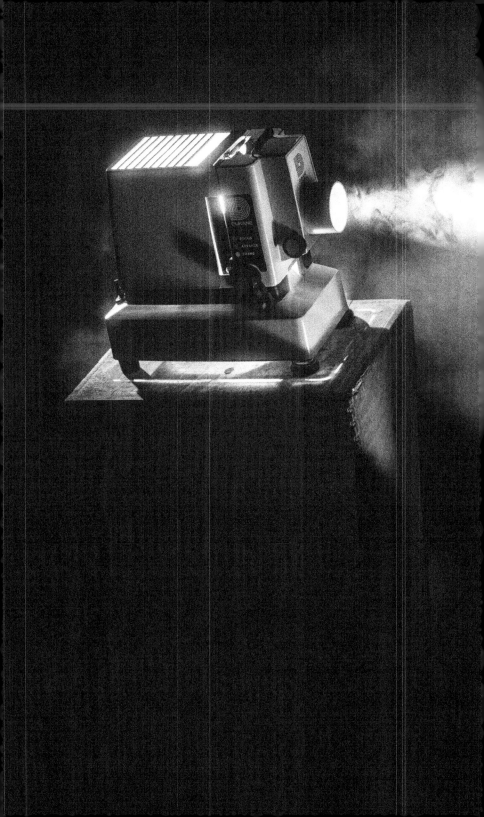

December 12th
∽

Chloe

Chloe wakes up with a jolt when her mom grabs the collar of her coat and shakes her.

"You have to get up, sweetie. We can't stay here."

For a moment, nothing makes sense to Chloe. She's not even sure where *here* is. Then her eyes adjust to the light, and the blurred fog behind her mom's back turns into snow-covered pine trees.

"What's ... going on?"

The answer comes not from her mom but from Abby, who is crouching slightly to their left, frantically rummaging through her backpack with her good arm.

"He's been here, Chloe," she says in a quivering voice. "He's been here, with us, tonight."

Chloe opens her mouth to ask what she's talking about, but she doesn't have time to say anything before Abby raises her hand and points toward the forest.

Chloe follows the direction of her finger—and has to stifle a scream.

In the shadows between the tree trunks, no more than sixty feet from where they slept, is a snowman. It's about the same height as the one she built with Abby, but other than that, there aren't many similarities.

Theirs had charm. This one looks like something out of a nightmare. The surface of the snow isn't smooth, like on other snowmen, but uneven and jagged, hinting that its creator was furious when he built it. Its eyes are deep holes, slightly slanted, so it looks as if the snowman is staring at Chloe with his head tilted. The mouth is shaped into a macabre grin with small, sharp stones for teeth.

"Come on," her mom says, after which she grabs Chloe's coat again, this time pulling her all the way up. "We have to get going. Abby, can you take the blanket?"

"On it."

"Good. And Dad? Where is he?"

"I'm over here."

Chloe looks in the direction of the sound and sees her dad standing on the opposite side of the clearing. He looks completely crazy. He is pale as a corpse, his eyes are constantly flickering from side to side, and he is clutching a large branch with both hands.

Only now does Chloe spot the second change that has been made in the snowy landscape during the night. Around the clearing and crisscrossing all over the ground in between the trees are footprints. One big mess of them, impossible to make head or tail of.

"You coming, Chloe?"

"Huh? Yeah, sorry. I'm coming."

Her head is still foggy from the abrupt awakening, and her body is stiff and weak, but Chloe tries her best to keep up as the rest of the family leave the clearing and make their way into the dense pine forest.

The next few hours of Chloe Gray's life unfold like a video clip stuck in a loop. Her constant focal point is the back of Abby's coat, and on either side of it, misty, gray tree trunks glide past at the edge of her field of vision.

Hardly any words are exchanged between the four members of the small family, but they groan and sigh in turn.

When her dad finally signals the others to stop, they have just come out of an overgrown area of the forest—and now find themselves on a flat piece of land that ends abruptly at the edge of a canyon. One that cuts them off from the straight route down the mountain.

"Fuck. Fuck, fuck, fuck!"

Alarmed by her dad's unexpected outburst, Chloe takes a few steps backward as the canyon catches his swear words and throws them mockingly back at him.

"Adam," their mom says as he lifts the large branch he's been dragging around and starts pounding it pointlessly into the ground. "You need to—"

"No, Beth," he hisses. "I don't need to do anything. I can't and I won't relax! It's too much. It's ... it's ..."

The gaze of his wide-open eyes moves away from her, landing on the forest behind them instead. He lifts the branch once more and holds it up in the air, the way a wizard might hold a staff while spewing a curse.

"ARE YOU OUT THERE?" are the words he shouts. "ARE YOU OUT THERE, YOU PSYCHO? ARE YOU HAVING FUN SCARING THE LIFE OUT OF US?"

Once again, the echo of his words travels up the mountain and down through the canyon before everything falls quiet again.

For a few seconds. Then the answer comes; a hoarse, mocking laugh that freezes the blood to ice in Chloe's veins. It starts low, not much louder than a whisper, then briefly increases in volume before suddenly disappearing again.

It came from everywhere and nowhere. Perhaps somewhere deep in the woods. Perhaps right behind them.

Horrified, Chloe seeks her dad's gaze, but his eyes bring no comfort. They're wide open, full of terror and disbelief. He hadn't expected an answer, and it's as if getting one caused something in his brain to short-circuit.

His lips begin to form a word that Chloe instinctively knows will be *RUN!* But before the sound reaches her ears, it's drowned out by another.

A devastating bang from somewhere inside the forest.

In its wake, Chloe sees her dad release his grip on the branch and press his hands against the gunshot wound in his thigh instead, while he senselessly staggers backward, straight toward the edge of the canyon.

And then past it.

The sight of her dad's bloody hand reaching out and grabbing nothing but air before disappearing below the edge is horrible. But it's the pause and the sound—the long second of silence, followed by a hollow thump as his body hits the bottom of the canyon—that sends Chloe into a full-blown state of shock.

Everything around her seems unreal and distorted, as if she is looking at it through a foggy window. Somewhere behind its glass, Abby and her mom are screaming, but the sound seems distant. Distorted, just like everything else.

Chloe also attempts to scream, but the sound gets stuck in her throat, refusing to come out.

A tremor moves through her legs. For a moment, she has no idea if it's coming from the ground beneath her feet or from somewhere inside her own body. Only when she registers the loud, whirring noise accompanying it does it fall into place for her.

She spins around in a semicircle and stares toward

the forest, while the sound rises, rises, rises, until a cloud of powdery snow comes rolling out from between the trees like a foaming wave in a stormy sea.

At the center of the cloud is the snowmobile. It's heading toward her—and it's not slowing.

Her brain knows she should jump aside, but her body is no longer under its command. It has been put out of action. Paralyzed. She is unable to do anything but close her eyes and turn her face away from the powdery snow spraying over her in the last milliseconds before the inevitable collision.

A forceful shove knocks the wind out of her and sends her stumbling to the ground, but ... it didn't come from in front of her. It came ... from the side?

She opens her eyes and sees her older sister's face. She is lying on the ground next to her. She has nuggets of snow in her hair and desperation in her eyes.

Behind Abby, their stalker—a man in a white ski suit—has brought the snowmobile to a halt just a few feet from the canyon's edge after carving a crescent-shaped trail in the snow. The sight of the trail tells Chloe that her older sister just saved her life by pushing her away. Because if she hadn't, Chloe would be at the bottom of the canyon right now. Together with her—

The thought is ripped to pieces when Abby suddenly screams and is pulled backward in one violent jerk. Chloe instinctively reaches out for her, but she only manages to graze the tips of her sister's fingers before Abby instead buries them in the snow in a useless attempt to hold on.

There's no point. The man is far too strong for her. He drags her a couple of feet backward, then moves his hands further up to get a better grip and pulls again. This time he lifts upward and steps sideways while he does it, which means Abby is swung around in a semicircle. And when he lets go, she is unable to stop on her own. She crashes into the rear of the snowmobile— and then falls limply to the ground.

For a moment, the man stands still in front of Abby, probably to see if she'll try to get up again. When she doesn't, he turns back to Chloe. He stares at her. She can't see his eyes or his mouth behind the goggles and ski mask, but she can *feel* his gaze. And she's also pretty sure he's smiling in there.

Now he takes a step in her direction. The snow creaks under his boots.

Behind the snowmobile, a shadow on the ground catches Chloe's attention, and she immediately knows what it is. *Who* it is.

And she also instinctively knows that she has just ruined their only chance by looking in that direction. Her eyes have warned *him* of what is about to happen.

Sure enough, he turns on his heels at the very moment her mom comes leaping forward—and he grabs her arms before she has the chance to bring her improvised club down on him. He gives her a knee in the stomach and twists her arms sideways, making the large branch, which now both their parents have, in vain, tried to use as a weapon, fall to the ground.

Chloe stares at the branch, telling herself to pick it up and defend her mom and sister. But she can't. She can't move. She can only sit here and cry like a whiny, useless baby.

"LET GO OF ME!" her mom screams, but the man doesn't. He keeps holding onto her wrists as he kicks her over and over until she gradually collapses and falls to the ground.

And falls silent.

When he finally lets go and dumps her mom's limp body in the snow next to Abby, Chloe still hasn't moved an inch. She just sits there, paralyzed by fear, staring at the stranger's ski goggles. At her own reflection, which now grows larger and larger in the glass with every step he takes toward her.

December 13th

᭡

Adam

A kaleidoscope, rotating and throwing him back into darkness every time he has fought his way a few yards forward. That is what Adam's universe has been reduced to. White ice crystals, speckled with tiny, dark red spots, that spin around and around nonstop. A hypnotic spiral.

Occasionally, he manages to get up on his feet, but a lot of the time he crawls. Most of the ... time.

Time? Does he have time?

Probably not much. He has a vague memory of trying to stop the bleeding during the night by tying his undershirt around the wound, but even if that worked, he has lost a large amount of blood already, and his consciousness comes and goes. Like waves rolling against a shore. And if he doesn't get his frozen body warm and treat his wound soon, one of the coming waves will be the last.

Heat and treatment. That should be his priority, he knows. But he has to get out of the canyon. He has to get back to the place where he was separated from his family. He needs to know what has happened to them.

Using that thought as the driving force, Adam makes another attempt at getting back on his feet. It triggers a burning pain in his side, possibly from a broken rib, and the kaleidoscope spins even faster, but he succeeds. He gets up, grabs one of the lower branches of a tree, and leans on it.

The next tree is about fifteen feet away. It might as well have been a hundred. Because everything is tilting. Rocking from side to side. It's like trying to walk across a soaking wet ship's deck in a storm. The only bright side is that the slope is less steep here and that he is approaching the top.

The finish line still feels like a mirage, though, as he has already had to walk very far through the canyon just to find a place where it was possible to get up without having to climb. And once up, he'll have to cover that distance one more time to get back to the place where he fell down.

He coughs, and a spray of small red droplets rains down on the snow in front of his boots.

"It doesn't matter," he whispers between chattering teeth. "Chloe, Abby, and Beth are all that matters. You just keep going."

With his eyes locked on the next pine tree, he lets go of the previous and staggers forward. The first six or seven feet, it's going okay. Then the tip of his boot bumps against something beneath the snow, and he tumbles forward.

The tree opens its arms, embracing him with stinging pine needles, whipping branches, and a shower of icy snow.

And there, hanging limply on the branches of the tree, Adam Gray slips back into the darkness.

He wakes to the sound of his own scream echoing through the canyon, and nothing has changed. Reality is still a nightmare, and he is still in the same spot, kneeling at the foot of a pine tree as if it were the statue of a deity he was praying to.

Wrong. Something *has* changed. The shadows of the trees are stretching to the left now. It's late afternoon, maybe early evening. Oh God, how many hours has he lost?

He puts one hand on the ground and grabs a cluster of the tree's thin branches with the other. Then he pulls.

It costs another cry of pain, but he gets up—and to his relief, the kaleidoscope has slowed down. It's still spinning, but not enough to knock him off his feet.

With his hands pressed against his thighs and his gaze fixed rigidly forward, he starts to walk. Every step is a struggle—not only against the knee-high piles of snow, but also against his own treacherous body, which pleads at him for another break. A rest that he knows he wouldn't be able to get up from.

Even as he crosses his first milestone—the edge of the canyon—he doesn't allow himself to pause. He staggers on in the direction of the next tree that he can lean on. Always the next tree.

He falls, yes. His face meets the icy surface of the snow again and again, but he keeps getting back up. He has no other choice. His family is somewhere out there. They're waiting for him. They need him.

And he needs them.

Seconds, minutes, and hours go by as Adam hikes along the edge of the canyon. At least he knows that he will be led back to where he fell if he just makes sure to keep it on his left-hand side. Then he can't miss it.

Or can he? He still has moments where he floats in and out of consciousness. What if he, in one of his half-awake moments, has walked right past the place without noticing it?

It's not very likely, but it's not impossible either—and that terrifies him. If he, enveloped in his own little bubble of fever, has missed their footprints.

Stop it. You're scared and confused, that's all. Breathe and pull yourself together.

He tries, but the only thing he achieves is an intense pain in his chest, making him feel as though the air he breathes is packed with tiny shards of glass.

His legs start to shake under him, and small spots

appear in his field of vision as he gradually sinks to his knees.

What if this is how it ends? What if you never get to see them again? If you've already seen them for the last time?

"Chloe ... Abby ... Beth," he mutters, not quite knowing why. Perhaps to keep his eye on the goal. Perhaps to convince himself that they're still real. "Chloe ... Abby ... Beth."

And what if they didn't get away from the maniac? If he got ahold of them?

This question hits Adam harder than the pain and exhaustion, harder than anything else, and from it he draws the strength to get back up and walk on.

Each step feels like an impossible task. Hell, each step *is* an impossible task, but he takes them anyway. Because he has to.

Half an hour later, it happens. He edges his way past two tree trunks, and as he steps out between them, he sees it.

Footprints in the snow. Lots of them, crisscrossing in random patterns in front of the canyon's edge. *Their* footsteps. Abby, Chloe, and Beth's footsteps. And his own.

But there are other tracks as well. There are two broad lines that come from the forest, form a semicircle close to the edge of the canyon, and from there disappear into the forest in the other direction. It has to be the snowmobile. Apart from this, there are prints from a pair of boots, which, judging by their size, belong to a grown man. But they aren't Adam's.

All of these things are deeply troubling, but there is one observation that shocks Adam more than anything else.

The trail from the snowmobile is the only thing that leads away from the site again. In other words, his family must have been driven away from the scene on it. By choice or by force.

A realization, as unbearable as it is indisputable, strikes him. He doesn't stand a chance. The trail is right there—two lines clearly etched into the surface of the snow—and it would likely lead him straight to his family ... if he were able to follow it to the end. The problem is that he won't get very far in his current state. He is hungry, he is thirsty, he has a fever, he is badly injured, and he has no strength left. If he could eliminate just one or two of these factors, he might have a small chance, but—

Wait. There is something. Or rather, there ... *was* something. Something his brain registered peripherally right before he stepped out between the two tree trunks. Something he caught a glimpse of but was distracted from when he saw the footprints.

A hallucination? Wishful thinking? Oh God, he hopes not.

With the very last of his strength, he turns around and staggers back to the two trees. Leaning against one of the trunks, he lets his gaze wander across the snow-covered forest floor until it finds what he is searching for.

The bushes *are* real—and so is the dark gray strap with red stripes he caught a fleeting glimpse of earlier. It's poking out between the thin, ice-covered branches at the bottom. And now, knowing what he's looking at, he can see the rest of it in there too.

Beth's backpack. She must have thrown it in there before ... before whatever happened, happened. But why? What was she hoping to achieve? That he would find it?

It doesn't matter, says a voice in his head, and Adam couldn't agree more. He has a first aid kit now, maybe even some food.

And above all else, he has hope.

December 14th

Beth

"I'm going to kill you."

Over the past twenty-four hours, Beth has uttered these words at every conceivable pitch and volume. She has screamed them, whispered them, sobbed them, hissed and sneered them.

Hundreds of variations have crossed her lips, and only a few times has she been certain that the recipient heard them. Because most of the time he's not in the room with her. He shows up with a dry sandwich when it's dinner time or when it's time to change the disgusting tin bucket in the corner that serves as her toilet.

He has done the latter twice. The first time, in anger and desperation, she tried to throw the contents of the bucket—piss, shit, and vomit—at him, but he was onto her. He smacked it out of her hands. So now, her already tiny isolation cell has been reduced to half its size if she wants to avoid sleeping in a puddle of her own feces.

"I know you can hear me out there. I'm going to kill you, you psycho."

In truth, she has no idea whether he's able to hear her. For all she knows, he could be on a weekend trip to Maryland right now. But if he's out there, if he's listening, he needs to know. Know how profound her hatred is. Know that she means every word.

She hasn't seen his face yet. It's hidden behind the reflective goggles and the white ski mask. In the dimness of her cell, it makes him look like a ghost every time the door opens and he enters with one of those cursed ham sandwiches in his hand. He also resembles the mannequins you sometimes see in shop windows. Smooth, white faces devoid of human features.

The door is made of metal, the walls of solid concrete, and there are no windows, so the faint orange glow from the ventilation grate up by the ceiling is the only light. Assuming that the room was built with the purpose of keeping people confined wouldn't be unreasonable.

Innocent people, like Beth. And like her daughters. Because Abby and Chloe are also here somewhere. Locked in a room like her. They have to be. Because if they're not here, it could mean that they've suffered the same fate as ...

In a flash, she sees it happen again. She sees Adam

staggering backward over the edge of the canyon, plunging into the abyss. This isn't the first time that scene has appeared on her inner movie screen. It has happened several times while she has been lying here in the dark, enveloped in the stench of her own shit— and each time the same question follows:

Was it instantaneous, or did he lie down there bleeding to death, unable to do anything but listen while some maniac abducted his entire family? Was that how Adam spent his last minutes?

"I'm gonna get out of here," she mumbles, scratching her nails across the walls of the corner she's curled up in. "I'm gonna get out, and when I do, I'll kill you. Just like you killed my husband."

It has become a mantra. A phrase she chants over and over again to keep her thoughts in a tight rein. To keep other thoughts out by focusing on the one.

She opens her eyes when a sound reaches her ear canal. Squeaking shoe soles on concrete somewhere outside the door. He's coming.

She fixes her gaze on the doorknob and crouches, pressing both hands against the floor, silently waiting with her veins full of adrenaline, like a predator lurking in tall grass.

She's not a fool. She realizes that she's not the predator here. But give her a chance, just the tiniest opening, and she'll—

A click and a heavy clank as the locking bolt shoots aside. Then the big metal door opens, and light burns her eyes like a shower of acid, robbing her of any advantage.

He enters, a tall silhouette in backlight, towering over her, peering down at her from behind the reflective glass of his goggles. He doesn't say anything, but she can see the fabric moving, and she can hear his breathing beneath the mask. It's rapid, almost moaning. As if standing on the heavy side of the balance of power excites him.

Her gaze slides down to the plate in his hands. It's the usual dry ham sandwich, but he carries the plate on his fingertips as if it were a silver platter with langoustine and fucking oysters.

And no, he's no fool either. It's a plastic plate. With a bit of luck, she could give him a mild scrape with its edge, but it's not going to cause any serious damage no matter how creative she gets. And when she gets water, it's served in a paper cup, which is about as useful a weapon in this situation as a beach ball in a needle shop.

Now, he takes a step forward and bends down to place the plate on the floor. The urge to lunge forward and knock it out of his hands is strong, but she suppresses it. She needs all the strength she can get if she is to get out of this. And strength requires food.

"Where are they?" she whispers instead. "Where are my girls?"

He lifts his head so that Beth comes face-to-face with herself in the glass of his goggles, and for a moment, it feels like he's actually going to answer. To talk to her for the first time. Then he tilts his head and pushes the plate. It slides across the floor with the sound of nails on a school blackboard, stopping a few inches from her feet.

"NO," Beth shouts as he starts to get up. "DON'T YOU DARE WALK AWAY! TELL ME WHAT YOU'VE DONE TO THEM! TELL ME, YOU BASTARD!"

He stops abruptly, and Beth shrinks, suddenly aware that her desperation and panic were allowed to take the wheel momentarily—and that it was a mistake.

She grimaces and holds her hands defensively up in front of her ... but the punches she anticipates never come. Instead, the man takes one step backward and one to the side, thus placing himself in the beam of light coming in from the doorway.

And standing there, he does something that Beth is going to remember for the rest of her days. He lifts one foot off the floor and runs a hand along the edge of its sole. Then he studies the hand for a second before turning it around so that Beth can see the palm.

And the red stripe running across it.

"W-what ... is that?" she hears herself ask, even though there isn't a shred of doubt in her mind. She knows exactly what it is. What she doesn't know—and doesn't dare to ask—is who it comes from.

He closes his hand, clenches it, as if to say he won't be taking any more questions. Then he turns his back on her, walks out of the room, and slams the metal door shut.

"You're going to pay for this," Beth hisses as darkness fills the cell again. "Do you hear me? I'm going to kill you, you psycho!"

December 15th

❦

Abby

Unlike her mom, Abby hasn't been isolated in a small, dark cell. She's in a large room with high ceilings. It's some kind of engine room, judging by the collection of old machines and generators at one end of the room. However, it seems like only a few of them are still in use, while the rest are covered in dust and spiderwebs, with occasional glimpses of rusty, oil-stained surfaces.

The air in here is also thick with the stench of old metal and oil. There is something else underneath as well. A nauseating smell that has Abby thinking of rotting wood beams, even though she hasn't seen any in here.

It *is* humid, though. That much is clear, as there are several small puddles of water scattered around the floor, and there is a constant, aggravating sound of droplets falling on the hard concrete. Along with the sparse lighting—some old fluorescent tubes that flicker irregularly and cast disturbing shadows on the walls—this creates an atmosphere of desperation and hopelessness.

So yes, the room is different, but that doesn't mean Abby enjoys more freedom than her mom, because along the concrete walls on both sides of the engine room runs a complex network of cables and rusty pipes. And Abby is tied to one of these pipes via a chain that only allows her about ten feet of freedom to move.

However, the main difference between her situation and her mom's—which is both a blessing and a curse —is that Abby has something that she doesn't.

Company. For Abby isn't the only one chained to one of the pipes in this eerie, reeking engine room. Chloe is here too. Like her older sister, she's wearing a heavy ankle shackle, the chain of which is only long enough to allow her to stand up and move a few yards. Her chain is locked to one of the pipes on the other side of the room ... which means that the two sisters can see and hear each other while at the same time being just too far apart to reach each other's hands.

At the moment, Chloe is sleeping. She does most of the time. Abby has a feeling that it's some sort of defense mechanism. That Chloe's body shuts down because it prefers the world of her subconscious rather than dealing with reality. It's painful to witness, and at first, Abby did everything in her power to try to comfort and distract her.

Gradually, though, she has started to think that her sister might be onto something with that strategy. After all, Chloe's breathing is way more relaxed when she sleeps. In the waking hours, she alternates between hyperventilating, sobbing, and asking questions that Abby is unable to answer, let alone think about, without it hurting.

Their abductor, the man with the ski goggles, would probably be able to answer most of those questions. He knows why he has taken them prisoner, and he knows what has happened to their mom, but he doesn't say anything. He limits himself to two forms of communication when there's something he wants Abby to do. He points and gestures—and if that doesn't work, he clenches his fists and takes a step toward her. Then she's suddenly able to push the empty plate back to him. Because no matter how much she desires to defy him, fear always wins in the end. She curls up and becomes small ... which she hates herself for. Especially when Chloe is watching. But what the hell is she supposed to do? The man is a psychopath, and even though she can't see his face, she can feel his revulsion when he looks at them.

Oh yeah, he hates them just as much as they hate him. You don't need a doctorate in body language to figure that out. Just look at the way he forces them to pee in a bucket while he uses the toilet behind the door in the back wall of the engine room. Hell, if their chains were ten feet longer, they'd be able to use that toilet too. But no, it has to be right out of their reach, just as they're close to each other but never close enough for physical contact.

In addition to the one leading to the toilet, there are two other doors in the room. One is the door he uses when he brings them food. It's over on Chloe's side, only down toward the other end of the wall.

The final one is a sliding door that hangs on a rusty metal rail. She has only seen him open it once, but that was also enough, because the brief glimpse she got of the room behind it was pretty disturbing. At least if the dark, glossy puddle on the floor is what her brain concluded it was.

On the other side of the room, Chloe starts twitching anxiously, almost as if Abby's thoughts had somehow made their way into her dream.

"Shh, you're alright, Chloe. You're just dreaming."

As soon as she has said the words, hopelessness latches on to Abby's heart like a malicious parasite, sucking all the strength out of her. Because it's a lie. *Nothing* is alright. Their dad is missing, probably dead, and their mom ... who knows?

He does, she thinks as tears blur her vision, transforming the door she's staring at into a surreal, dancing Rorschach shape. *The psycho knows.*

In the first confused second, Abby thinks the scream that woke her up came from Chloe. But when she looks over there, she sees Chloe sitting on her knees, appearing just as mystified as herself.

And when Abby's brain rewinds and re-analyzes the sound, she realizes that it couldn't possibly have been Chloe. Because the scream came from a man.

"What is happening?" Chloe asks in a voice on the verge of breaking. "Oh God, Abby. What's going on out there?"

Another scream—louder, and most definitely closer—interrupts Abby's response and makes the hairs on her arms stand. Not least because she's pretty sure that she caught some words hidden within the animalistic scream this time around.

Please, not again! I'm begging you!

Instinctively, she looks at Chloe to see if she heard the hidden plea as well. It doesn't look like it. She looks upset, but no more than before.

New sounds emerge. Footsteps, scraping, bashing, and muffled sobs. It sounds like it's coming from the other side of the wall on Chloe's side.

No sooner has Abby finished that thought than the door is opened over there. No, that is too mild a description. It's *torn* open, after which their abductor comes marching into the room.

His one hand points ominously at Abby as if to say: *not a fucking word!* His other hand is clasping the coat of the elderly man he is dragging behind him across the floor.

"Chloe, don't look!" Abby exclaims as the man on the floor gets far enough into the room for her to see him clearly. Sadly, it's too late. Chloe has seen him— and the sight has drained all color from her face.

The man on the floor is Bill, their holiday host. The last time Abby saw him was when he said goodbye after giving them the key to the cabin. Back then, he shook their dad's hand out in the driveway and then waved to her and Chloe, who stood behind the window in the living room. Bill wouldn't be able to do either of those things anymore, given that his hands have been reduced to two crooked lumps of flesh at the end of his forearms. They're wrapped in some kind of bandages, but they don't cover much, and Abby can easily see that all the fingers have been amputated on his right hand, while the left has only the thumb left.

In one place, the bandage is completely open, so she can see the exposed wound behind it. Or rather, she can see a cracked, grayish-black crust. Because naturally, the maniac with the ski goggles has made sure to close the wound again by scorching it.

Now, Bill's eyes find her, and slowly—*chillingly slowly*—recognition dawns in them. And with it comes panic.

"No, no, no, they're just kids. What have you done?"

he mumbles, looking up at the man with the goggles, who answers him with the usual silence.

Bill's gaze drifts over to Chloe and, from there, back to Abby. His eyes are wide, desperate. They're the eyes of a prey animal on the run. He opens his mouth to say something to her, a warning of some kind, judging by the look on his face, but before he can do so, the man with the goggles plants a boot heel on the sad remains of Bill's left hand and steps on it, hard.

In an instant, the words turn into a scream—and when it has died down, Bill's quavering lips stay sealed while his tormentor drags him on through the engine room.

Their destination is the room behind the sliding door.

"Make him stop! Please, make him stop!"

The first few times her little sister shouted those words, Abby thought Chloe was talking to her. She no longer believes that. Because Chloe isn't looking at her. Chloe isn't looking at *anybody*. She has her eyes closed, and she covers both ears, while those same words pour out of her mouth in a constant stream.

Abby has no idea what the official symptoms of shock are, but she's pretty sure that Chloe is showing at least a few of them. She is crying uncontrollably, and her whole body is shaking.

Abby is shaking too. Especially her hands. She tries to steady them by wedging them between the floor and her shins while she kneels, but it doesn't really work, and it hurts her fingers.

At least you still have all your fingers.

As an eerie extension of that thought, another cry of pain emerges from the room behind the sliding door. It's Bill, but he hardly even sounds like a human being anymore. He sounds like the crows who always sat on the power lines outside their grandma's house in the countryside.

The screaming continues for a while—it could be two minutes, it could be twenty, Abby has no idea—and then it suddenly stops. It happens without warning; in the middle of a scream and just as abruptly as when you press *Stop* on a remote control and kill a music track.

The ensuing silence is only broken by Chloe and Abby's ragged, uneven breathing, along with a few short thudding sounds from behind the sliding door.

"Is he ... dead?" Chloe whispers.

Abby makes a strained swallowing motion and states, with a headshake, that she has no idea.

Now, the door slides aside with a shrill screech, and the man with the ski mask steps back into the engine room. Behind him, Bill lies on the floor, motionless and limp like a pile of dirty laundry. One of his boots and the sock underneath have been removed. So have a couple of his toes. Where they were is now a wound, paved with the same charred surface that Abby saw on his hands.

Whether he is unconscious or dead, she can't determine. A part of her hopes—for his sake—for the latter.

After casting one last glance in the direction of his victim, the man with the ski goggles goes into the bathroom. He is probably going in there to wash the blood off his hands because they're completely—

It's like an explosion in Abby's brain when the first real idea of how they could escape hits her.

She looks down at her ankle shackle. Would it work? The answer is *maybe* ... and *maybe* is more than enough justification for trying.

Her gaze leaves the ankle shackle and instead moves up to the toilet door. There it'll remain until it opens again. She is hoping to confirm one thing, and—

Now it happens. The door swings open, and ... yes. The soap is on the sink next to the tap. And it's a bar of soap. Not some wall-mounted dispenser, but a small, smooth bar of soap in solid form. If they can get ahold of it somehow, they may be able to use it to free themselves from the ankle shackle.

Of course, there is the obvious problem, that the man with the ski goggles always closes the toilet door behind him—which he does now as well. At this very moment, however, it doesn't matter.

Because for the first time since waking up in this horrible room, Abby feels a glimmer of hope. And she intends to focus on it with all her heart.

Just like she does now ... as she catches one last glimpse of Bill's lifeless body before the man with the white ski mask closes and locks the sliding door and then strolls out of the engine room as if nothing has happened.

December 16th

Chloe

"I'm not exactly loving it either, Chloe, but we have no other choice."

Somewhere deep down, Chloe knows that her older sister is right. But it being the only solution doesn't mean she has to love it, does it? And she really doesn't. She hates the idea that Abby wants to distract the man with the goggles the next time he comes out of the bathroom. That's what Abby calls it; *distract* him. Yet, Chloe knows that it really means that she's going to make him angry.

"Can't we just try the handle again?"

Abby shakes her head and sighs.

"We can't pull it far enough down," she says. "You know that. We have tried and tried and tried. If we keep trying, I'll have no strength left to get the soap out, even if we got the door open. And that's a *big* if."

Chloe looks down at the long, improvised rope

twisting like a snake on the floor in front of Abby's feet. It's made with pieces of their clothes, tied together; Abby's sweater and coat, and Chloe's shirt.

In theory, it should work, but every time they've managed to get the knot at the end of the rope wedged behind the door handle, they haven't been able to pull it all the way down because the angle is too sharp. At least that's what Abby says.

"I don't like it. What if he's ... mean to you?"

Images flicker by on her retina—Bill being dragged across the floor, unable to fight back because his hands have been turned into two useless lumps of flesh, her dad's confused face just before he tumbled over the edge of the canyon—and tears begin to run down her cheeks.

"Listen," Abby says in a voice whose shaky timbre makes her determined facade crack, revealing how scared she actually is. "I'm going to do it no matter what, but I'd prefer that you, um ... that you accept it, okay?"

"Why does it matter if you're going to do it anyway?"

"It just does, Chloe! Okay?"

A pause. Chloe spends it with her eyes fixed on the concrete floor. Then she nods slowly.

"Say it," Abby insists.

"I ... accept your plan. Happy now?"

Abby responds with a faint smile and a nod. Then she motions for Chloe to move toward the center of the floor.

"Come here and help me untie this. We've got to get our clothes back on before he comes."

～

Why has he been in there for so long? Chloe thinks nervously when she hears the toilet flush behind the door and sees her older sister pull off one of her boots over on the other side of the engine room. *Does he know that something is wrong? Could he tell from looking at us? At me?*

She tries to catch Abby's attention by waving her hand, but Abby's gaze is fixed on the door, and it doesn't move an inch. She looks crazy.

Crazy, but also terrified.

"Hey, Abby," Chloe whispers. "I've changed my mind, I—"

Too late. The handle moves downward, the door opens, and Abby's arm is already pulled back.

"HEY!" she shouts, hurling her boot at him. "ARE YOU HAVING FUN KEEPING US TRAPPED IN HERE? YOU'RE FUCKING SICK, YOU KNOW THAT? ASSHOLE!"

The boot hits the man's thigh and falls to the floor in front of him. He glances down at it, then at Abby—and in a terrible moment, Chloe is struck by déjà vu. It's Abby's outburst of anger that does it. Because Abby sounds exactly like their dad when he stood at the canyon's edge and shouted into the woods just before he was shot.

And in that terrible moment, Chloe knows that it will happen again. That the man with the ski goggles is going to take her sister away from her, just like he took her dad.

Now it begins. He takes a step toward Abby and raises his index finger in a threat that can't be misunderstood. *One more word and you'll regret it.*

Chloe holds her breath and stares at her older sister, worried what she is going to do. For a moment, it seems to be nothing ... but then, as the man starts to turn back toward the toilet door, the mad look of desperation re-emerges in Abby's eyes.

"OH MY, YOU SURE ARE A TOUGH GUY, HUH?" she shouts, her voice shrill as that of a small child. "THREATENING A GIRL HALF YOUR SIZE. WHAT A REAL MACHO MAN!"

"Abby, n-no!" Chloe stammers, but once again it's too late. The man is already by her sister, and now, he grabs the arm she is trying to protect herself with.

Abby screams in pain as he twists her arm around, forcing her to lie with her chest and one cheek pressed against the floor. With his free hand, he starts punching her in the side, just below the ribs, causing her to let out a series of involuntary gurgling sounds.

"Leave her alone," Chloe begs, but the man couldn't care less about her appeals. He continues to hammer his hand into Abby's side—and when that starts to bore him, he grabs her hair instead and starts banging her head against the concrete floor.

Chloe shuts her eyes, but it doesn't help. In the darkness behind her eyelids, the sound is amplified, making every clash between Abby's head and the hard surface of the floor roll over her like a thunderclap.

Tha-whomp, tha-whomp, tha-womp.

Suddenly, it's over, and the sound of her own gasping breath is the only thing reaching Chloe's ears. She opens her eyes and jerks back in fear as she sees the man walking straight toward her. But he doesn't stop. He turns left, brushes past her, and then disappears out the door, slamming it shut behind him.

"Abby?" Chloe whispers. "Abby, are you ..."

Her voice dies out as Abby slowly lifts her head a few inches off the floor, exposing a cheek that is bluish, swollen, and filled with small red fissures. It looks freaky. Her skin seems ... *cracked.* Just like the faces on Chloe's old dolls in the end before her mom finally told her to throw them out.

"Deh hee worhk?"

"What? I'm sorry, I can't understand what you're saying."

"Deh hee worhk?" Abby repeats, raising a trembling finger on one hand to point behind her in the direction of the toilet.

"Oh, if it worked? Yeah, um ... yeah, he forgot all about the door. It's still open."

Abby's quivering index finger is replaced with a

thumb. Then she moans, lets her head drop back to the
floor, and starts crying.

Chloe opens her mouth but closes it again without
saying anything. It can wait. Abby deserves a break.

They won't get many attempts. Not without resting in
between them, at least. Because Abby has done
nothing more than to get ready for the first throw, and
her face is already contorted in pain. The man in the
ski mask didn't hold back.

If she could, Chloe would have volunteered to take
over. The problem is that she sits on the side that the
toilet door opens toward, so she can see neither the
sink nor the soap. And so, it's big sister to the rescue
again.

Their improvised rope consists of the same ele-
ments as before—Chloe's shirt and Abby's sweater and
coat—but they've tied a couple of extra knots at the
end this time, hoping it will make it easier to pull the
soap down.

To the floor, she adds inside her head. *If it ends up in
the sink, it's game over.*

"Elbow, forearm, wrist," Abby whispers at the other
side of the room, after which she bites her lower lip
and pulls her arm back.

Hearing those words give Chloe a lump in her throat.

It was a mantra their dad taught them when they first started playing basketball together. A way to make sure they had the right technique before throwing the ball.

"You can do it, Abby," she stammers.

Abby nods without taking her eyes off the target. Then she slings her arm forward. The rope shoots through the air, twisting like a snake. It hits the door-frame with three consecutive thumps—one for each knot—before falling limply to the floor.

"Damn it," Abby mumbles and starts to pull back the rope. She does it with slow, strained movements, pausing several times to catch her breath. During one of these pauses, it actually looks like she is about to pass out.

"Maybe we should ..." Chloe starts, but Abby sends her a look that silences her.

"I can do it," she hisses. "I just ... I just need a minute, okay?"

Chloe nods, holding her hands up in front of her.

Abby takes her minute—and then another. After that, she gets up, picks up the rope, takes aim, and throws it once more.

Chloe follows the three knots that make up the head of the symbolic snake as it darts forward and vanishes through the doorway.

As before, there are three thumps as the knots encounter resistance—but this time, three more follow right after. Since she can't see into the bathroom, she has to read the reaction on her sister's face to know what the three extra thumps mean.

And Abby is smiling.

"You got it?"

"I freaking got it."

With pursed lips, Abby begins to pull the rope back, and sure enough; with the second-to-last knot comes a small, cream-colored bar of soap. She picks it up and stares at it with teary eyes while she lets out a sound that lies somewhere in between the chuckle of a madman and a desperate sob. Then she pulls off her boot and her sock and starts smearing soap on the areas above and below the shackle.

"It's too dry," she mumbles when the first attempt to pull off the chain fails. "I need some water."

She looks at the floor around her—and finding that none of the small puddles are within her reach, she grows desperate and starts spitting on her hands. This doesn't change the result, though. Her shackle stays where it is.

"Let me try," Chloe says. "I don't think mine is as tight as yours."

"Give me a sec. I haven't given up yet."

After those words, Abby spits on her palms once more and rubs them on the soap bar. This time, foam appears between her fingers ... but it doesn't help much. No matter how hard she pulls, the shackle doesn't get past her heel. And she does pull hard. So hard that the white foam turns pink when her skin tears.

"Come on, Abby," Chloe says. "Let me give it a try. I'm telling you, mine is looser."

Abby stares at her hesitantly for a moment. Then she pushes the soap across the floor to her. Chloe picks it up, removes her footwear, and starts rubbing the soap against her skin. It breaks off in small flakes that resemble scales.

Unlike Abby, Chloe does have water within reach. It lies in a small, pear-shaped puddle on the floor below the pipe she is chained to. She places her hand flat in the water, soaking her palm and fingers. Next, she grabs her foot and moistens the soap scales. It foams a lot more than it did with Abby. It almost looks as if she has just pulled her foot out of a foamy hot tub.

Except it isn't hot. Her foot is cold, and the metal feels icy against her fingers as she grabs the shackle and pushes it downward.

Her foot hurts. On the *inside*, in the bones. So much so that she can't help but grind her teeth as she presses again. It's either that or screaming. And it's too dangerous to scream, in case—

A wet squelch sounds, and before she has time to react, her bent leg shoots upward like a tightly wound spring suddenly released. The collision between her knee and jaw floods her vision with flickering spots and sends her toppling backward, so instead of sitting on her butt, she ends up flat on her back.

For a moment, that's all she registers. That—and the rusty taste of blood in her mouth. Then she hears Abby say:

"You did it! You actually did it, Chloe!"

Chloe blinks a few times and looks down at herself. Abby is right; she is free from the ankle shackle.

"Hurry up," Abby says, waving her hand. "Come over here and help me!"

Chloe nods, then grabs the soap and crawls over to Abby with it in her hand. She doesn't use it right away, though. In fact, she just opens her hand and drops it on the floor when she gets there so she has both arms free to embrace her sister.

"Just give it up, Chloe."

"No."

"I'm serious. It's no use."

"So am I. I'm not going anywhere without you."

"We don't have time to fight about it. I—"

"Then shut up."

"Chloe ..."

"No!"

"Look at me, Chloe!"

Chloe doesn't want to. Abby's green eyes are the last thing in the world she wants to look at right now because she knows exactly what she's going to find in them.

Abby leaves her no choice. She grabs both sides of Chloe's head and turns it upward until she can no longer escape eye contact.

"I can't," Chloe cries. "I can't just leave you here."

"Of course you can," Abby whispers, pressing her forehead against Chloe's. "Besides, you're not actually leaving me. I mean, you're coming back, right? You're just getting help."

"But what if he—"

"You don't need to worry about that at all. You only have to worry about getting out of here and finding a phone or something so you can call for help, okay?"

Chloe closes her eyes and nods. A part of her wishes they had never gotten ahold of that stupid bar of soap. Because it's not fair. Getting so close to freedom, only to see it dissolve right in front of them like a fata morgana in a desert. And her being able to get free of the chain, while her older sister can't, somehow just makes it worse. Because from this moment on, whatever happens will be on Chloe's shoulders. Her actions will determine Abby's fate.

"Now, I want you to listen carefully," Abby says, grabbing her shoulders. "Can you do that?"

Chloe wipes her cheeks with her sleeve and responds with a solemn nod.

"Good," Abby says. "When you get out, I mean all the way outside, you have to *run*. No hesitating and no looking back. Houses, roads, telephone poles—anything that looks like it could lead to cities and people—that's your compass, okay?"

"O-okay."

"But *not* in here," Abby says sternly, gesturing toward the building that surrounds them. "As long as you're inside this place, you take it easy, okay? You sneak around without making any noise, and if you hear any sounds, you hide. Voices too. Even if ..."

She hesitates for a moment and then clears her throat.

"Even if it's me or Mom you're hearing."

"But—"

"Promise me, Chloe! Promise me you won't come back until you've found help."

For a long time, Chloe does nothing but stare at her sister while biting her lower lip and breathing through her nose in small, short puffs. Then she nods, slowly and reluctantly.

"I want to hear you say it," Abby insists.

"Fine! I promise, okay? Is that what you want to hear?"

Abby doesn't answer that. She simply leans forward and plants a kiss on Chloe's forehead. After this, she gives her a gentle nudge in the direction of the door.

"Take care of yourself, okay?"

"I will."

"Good. Now get on out of my room, sis."

December 17th

Adam

The first snowflake—a delicate, symmetrical miracle—falls softly from a silvery sky. Adam's eyes observe it, watch it closely as it twirls in the wind, as if it's dancing to a melody only it can hear.

With bated breath, he studies the small, star-shaped ice crystal as it floats past his face, and his heart is filled with a quiet awe.

The snowflake continues its elegant journey downward until it lands gently at its destination; an outstretched palm.

Abby's outstretched palm.

For a moment, the snow crystal lies there, sparkling like a small diamond in the light of the winter sun. Then the heat from her skin begins to melt it.

But that's okay, because Abby is laughing. A bright and joyful sound that echoes through the cold air. Also, there are more snowflakes on the way. They're pouring down from the sky now, surrounding them, *enveloping* them, as Abby looks up at him. Her eyes are large and shining, filled with a mixture of wonder and joy.

Abby is three years old, so this isn't the first time in her life she has seen snow. But it's the first time she looks at it with such an expression in her eyes—and it fills Adam with a feeling of love so strong that it almost hurts. Love for her, and for her mom, who is leaning against his shoulder with her arm around his waist.

This is the first time Adam has the thought and feels its undeniable truth in his heart.

He would *die* for his family. He would give his life for theirs, without hesitation and without reservation.

Many years have passed since that day and that moment. Now, Adam is staring at another first snowflake falling from the sky. Yet, this little dancing ice crystal doesn't feel like a miracle from the hand of nature. It feels like a threat, a reminder that time is running out. That his only hope—a trail in the snow that has already been halfway erased by the wind— will soon be completely buried under the white blanket of oblivion.

His legs feel heavy, every movement a battle against the icy cold that bites through his clothes, paralyzing his muscles. His breathing is unstable, and each inhalation causes a painful flame to flare up in his chest.

White dots fill his field of vision now, swirling

around him, taking away a little bit of his hope every time one lands on the ground.

How long has he been out here, staggering forward, trying to keep his gaze locked on the rest of the snow-mobile's tracks in the snow? Three days? Four? Five? He has no idea because it all flows together. It feels like he's being helplessly swept along in a river of light and darkness—and it's not just the nights bringing darkness. For even though, by some stroke of luck, the bullet passed clean through, allowing him to get back on his feet with the help of the first aid kit in his backpack after about a day, he's still badly injured. Still drifting in and out of consciousness. At one point, he collapsed while the sun was high in the sky—and when he opened his eyes again, the moon had taken its place.

They melt so fast, Dad, Abby from the past whispers, and that one second where his focus falls back to the three-year-old version of his daughter is enough for him to lose control of his legs and tumble forward. He sinks into the snow, and his knees hit something hard —a rock or a tree stump—with a creaking sound.

"I ... can't," he moans, his voice almost drowned out by the howl of the wind. He lets himself fall forward so that his forehead meets the surface of the snow. The cold spreads to the rest of his face, a strange caress in the endless pain. His eyes slip shut, and exhaustion drags him down into darkness as the snow continues to fall around him. *On* him. He is going to witness his own burial, not under ground, but beneath a pile of white ice crystals.

And it won't be a hero's end. He won't get to give his life for them. He won't get to save his family. He is going to die alone, not knowing their fate, and he is too weak to fight it.

He allows it to happen, allows the snow to cover him, while his thoughts get slower and slower. As if they are also freezing.

In the dark, Abby reappears. Her shining eyes and her outstretched hand. Her tiny, pink palm and the little crystal that melts on it.

Chloe is there too. She is standing next to her older sister, like her, captivated by the dance of the snowflakes. Her lips are spread in a smile, and from them, a gentle, melodic laughter flows.

Chloe's presence makes no sense because it's still the little three-year-old version of Abby he is seeing ... which means that her little sister hasn't been born yet.

Sense or no sense, Adam doesn't care. If this image —his daughters in awe of the snow waltz—is the last thing he gets to see, so be it.

Slowly, the image begins to fade, and soon the distant echo of their laughter is all that lingers in the darkness.

No.

There is also something else. A shrill, whirring noise, buzzing in the background. It sounds like an angry wasp trapped under a plastic cup. Or rather;

that's what it sounds like at first, but the noise continues to increase in volume until he can almost feel it buzzing in his bones. It's as if it's shaking him. As if it's trying to—

The realization hits him like an electric shock, and he is pulled back to the present with a gasp.

Confused and weak, but with adrenaline burning in his veins, he fights his way onto all fours and looks in the direction of the sound as it gradually fades out and disappears again.

Did he imagine it? Has the cold and the distress finally pushed him all the way over the edge to madness? Did his own brain create the sound as a last desperate attempt to get him to continue despite the tracks in the snow being gone?

No. It *did* happen. It was real. He heard it, somewhere on the other side of the wall of trees towering in front of him.

The snowmobile.

December 18th

Beth

Footsteps. He's back.

Beth sits up, anxiously staring at the doorknob, unable to decide whether she hopes it will be pressed down or not.

Her hatred hasn't diminished. That's not the reason. But her abductor hasn't brought her food and water for a long time, maybe several days, and her body feels like it's being eaten away from the inside.

Everything hurts; her muscles, her bones, her guts. Each and every cell is screaming for nourishment. And it's not that he hasn't been close, because at least a couple of times she's heard him driving to and from the site on the snowmobile. The sound of its engine is shrill enough to find its way into her cell via the ventilation duct.

More footsteps. She opens her mouth to ask if he's

out there, but her throat is coated with gravel, and the only thing crossing her lips is a dry, squeaky cough.

The footsteps stop. Right outside the door, judging by the sound. Suddenly Beth is overcome with indignation. Is he just standing out there, listening to her cough? Is he chuckling behind his mask while she is withering away due to lack of fluids?

In that thought, she finds the strength to crawl forward and kick the door while dragging words up through the graveled tunnel of her throat.

"Are you having fun? Does it turn you on to listen to me coughing myself to death?"

Silence. Not that it comes as a surprise. By now, she's well aware that the freak doesn't—

"Mom?"

Beth stiffens and curls up. It's a trick. It *has to* be. Somehow, he is changing his voice to fool her.

"Is that you, Mom? Are you in there?"

It's not him. It's Chloe, her voice fragile and full of the same wary doubt that Beth feels. She's also afraid that it's a trap.

"Oh my God, Chloe," Beth stammers. "Yes ... yes, it's me."

For a while, there's no answer, but she can hear Chloe's breathing on the other side of the door. It's uneven, wheezing. She's crying. So is Beth now.

"Mom, h-he's still got Abby," Chloe sobs. "I tried to get her free, I really did, but I couldn't, and now I can't get back to her, and I can't get out either. I'm ..."

"It's okay, sweetie. Breathe. Deep breaths. Can you do that for me?"

"Y-yeah ... yes, I think so."

"Good. We'll do it together. In ... and out. In ... and out. That's better, isn't it?"

"Uh-huh."

"Okay. Then I want you to do something for me, okay? I'd like you to look at the lock on the door and see if you can open it. Can you do that?"

For a while, it's completely quiet on the other side of the door. In fact, Beth is just about to ask if Chloe is still out there when there is a loud clank as the locking bolts push aside.

The door opens with a screech, and Beth's heart bursts.

"Oh God, sweetie," she moans as the girl falls into her embrace. "I was afraid that ..."

She never completes the sentence. Instead, she squeezes tighter and kisses Chloe on top of her head. Her hair is messy, and it smells of oil.

For a while, they sit like that, mother and daughter in a tight embrace. Then reality suddenly hits Beth again, and she pulls back a bit so she can make eye contact with Chloe.

"We can't stay here. If he comes back—"

"He's not here," Chloe interrupts. "He left last night. I saw him go out, and I heard the snowmobile as he drove off. He hasn't come back yet."

"You *saw* him?"

"Yeah, I ... I can't get out, so I've had to hide. But there's this storage room he never uses, and that's where I've been most of the time."

"How long?" Beth asks in a quivering voice. "How long have you been out there alone, Chloe?"

"I don't know. A few days, I think. But I have food. There's a room, kind of like a kitchen, but not quite, where he hides the food. And when he's away, I sneak in there and grab some."

This image—her little girl having to sneak around to get food and avoid bumping into the maniac who is holding them captive—is too much for Beth. She clenches her hand, brings it up to her mouth, and bites her knuckles until the pain pushes it aside.

When she is able to speak again, Beth grabs Chloe's shoulders and looks at her.

"You said you were locked up together with Abby. Can you show me where?"

"I can't," Chloe says in a voice revealing that she is on the verge of breaking down in tears again. "I can't get back to her. The room she's in is at the end of a long corridor, and when I came out from it, I didn't know that the door could only be opened from the inside. On the other side, it needs a key, and ..."

"He's the only one who has it," Beth finishes for her.

Chloe nods and swallows with a pained expression on her face.

"It's not your fault, sweetie," Beth says, stroking her hand over her cheek. "You couldn't know."

Chloe nods again but doesn't look very convinced.

"And the other direction?" Beth asks. "Have you found a way out of here?"

"I think so," Chloe confirms. "But it's locked too."

Beth rubs her face and lets out a heavy sigh. Then she nods decisively.

"Okay, we can figure this out," she says. "We just have to take it one problem at a time—and the first thing is to find Abby and get her free. Can you take me to that door?"

Chloe nods, after which they both get up and leave what has been her mom's prison cell for the past several days.

The claustrophobic cell was bad, but the rest of the place isn't much better. It's a creepy maze of shadowy corridors and rooms, the walls of which are covered in cracked paint and large humidity stains that form unsettling images in the mind of a nervous viewer.

Without a doubt, Beth would lose her bearings within minutes if she were on her own, but Chloe confidently guides her along, whilst half-open doors, posters, and bulletin boards with discolored notes rush past at the edges of Beth's vision.

Whatever this place is, two things can be determined with certainty: it used to be a workplace—most of the rooms behind the doors contain office furniture

—and it no longer is, given that everything is covered in mold and dust.

The elaborated answer comes as they round a corner and encounter a spiral staircase. For on the wall next to the stairs is another dusty bulletin board, and on it hang two notes. One declares that staff meetings take place every Monday at 10 a.m., which doesn't make her much wiser, but the other is a green sheet of paper announcing that ...

ECHO DEFENSE RADIO STATION CELE-BRATES 40TH ANNIVERSARY!

Come and join us in celebrating four decades of successfully protecting our communications.

The party will take place on June 12th, 1985, at 18:00 in the main hall.

—Management

An abandoned radio station. Of course. A building of this size, hidden away in the mountains—what else could it be?

"It's right down here," Chloe says as she steps out onto the first step, making it squeak under her weight. "We're almost there."

Beth grabs the cold railing and follows. Her footsteps also trigger the sound of screeching metal—and every single time, it makes her frown. Partly because the sound is unpleasant, and partly because it's louder than she'd like it to be.

After reaching the bottom, Chloe leads her out into a medium-sized room filled with dusty desks and office chairs. Here, she stops and points.

"That's the door I was talking about. The corridor leading down to Abby is behind it. It's locked."

Beth lets her gaze drift over the door and along its frame. It looks sturdy. Too sturdy.

"You said you were able to open it from the other side, right?"

Chloe nods, and Beth's gaze moves upward. She is hoping to find one particular thing, and ... yes. It's there. A ventilation grate. Old and rusty, like everything else in the building ... but big enough for a girl of Chloe's size.

"Help me with this," Beth says, grabbing the edge of one of the desks. "It'll make too much noise if I drag it."

For a moment, Chloe looks confused, but when her mom directs her attention up to the grate with a nod, the dots connect. She grabs the table, and they carry it together, placing it on the floor underneath the grate.

After climbing onto the table, Beth raises her hand and examines the narrow slats on the front of the grate. The once white paint is almost completely peeled off, exposing the raw metal underneath. In the corners are dark gray lumps of dust, and below them, small threads of cobweb dangle, swaying slightly in the weak air current.

The slats are close together, but not too close to prevent Beth from squeezing her fingers in between them and grabbing hold.

She pulls, and the two slats she is holding bend slightly downward. The grate itself, however, isn't going anywhere.

"I need something I can use to break it loose," she sighs. "Do you see anything?"

Chloe glances around the room and shakes her head.

"There are only chairs and tables. But there was a toolbox in the room where I was hiding. I can run back and—"

"No!" Beth says. "You're not going anywhere. Give me, um ... give me that."

"This one?" Chloe asks, pointing to an old desk chair. "What are you going to do with that?"

"The backrest. It's adjustable—and that means it can also be taken off completely."

Chloe stares at the backrest as if evaluating the truth in that claim. Then she nods and lifts the chair up from the floor.

Beth takes it, locates the adjustment mechanism, and begins to turn it. Once the backrest is sufficiently loose, she pulls it off and hands it to Chloe. Then she raises the office chair up above her head, jams its back support—which now consists solely of a metal rod—in between the slats of the ventilation grate, and presses the lower part of the chair up against the ceiling next to it.

Her plan is to use it as a crowbar to pull the grate loose ... and it works. The grate creaks, and after a few attempts, there is a loud crack. The entire left side gives way and is released from the ceiling, raining a shower of gray dust onto the floor.

"It's working!" Chloe exclaims below her, and despite the gravity of the situation, Beth can't help but smile as she moves the backrest to the opposite side and repeats the process.

The other side is easier. A single, heavy pull is all it takes for the grate to come off completely and fall down on the table with a clunk.

"Alright, sweetie," Beth says, looking down at her daughter. "You're up."

Seeing the soles of Chloe's boots disappear into the darkness of the air duct so soon after reuniting with her pains Beth.

There just isn't any other way. The duct is too narrow for her to crawl through, and time is against them.

"You can do it, sweetie," she whispers. "Do you see any other grates up there?"

"I think so," Chloe replies, her voice tense and fragile. "There is some kind of light up ahead, at least."

While speaking, the girl slowly inches forward in the narrow duct, causing it to rattle ominously—and Beth's heart to pound in her chest.

"It'll be fine," Beth whispers, in part to Chloe, in part to herself.

The rattling noises continue as the seconds creep by, and slowly, doubt starts growing in Beth's mind. And with it comes guilt. Because what if the channel narrows somewhere up there and Chloe ends up getting stuck? Or if she gets claustrophobic and freezes in place? If she ends up sitting in there, paralyzed by fear and unable to move, while Beth can't do anything but—

A crash, loud and metallic, reverberates through the air duct, startling Beth so badly that she almost loses her balance and falls off the desk.

The crash is followed by a series of similar but more muffled noises—and as she listens closer, Beth realizes that it's not just the volume that makes a difference. It's also their origin. Because these noises aren't coming from the air duct above her. They're coming from the corridor behind the locked door.

Her gaze drifts toward it, and just as she focuses on the doorknob, there is a click.

The door opens, and there is her daughter. Little Chloe, dirty, pale, and frightened, but at the same time more adult and tough-looking than ever.

"Hurry up," Chloe whispers, pointing down to the

end of the corridor. "Abby's down there. Right around the corner."

Beth nods and hurries down from the desk, after which she runs over to Chloe, who is still holding the door open. Passing her, she takes the time to lean down and kiss her on the forehead.

"You're the best, sweetie."

Chloe replies with a frail smile before taking her mom's hand and leading her down the long corridor.

As they round the corner and spot the door to the engine room, Beth's heart is filled with something she hasn't felt in a while.

Hope. Sparkling and intoxicating. It washes through her, cures her fatigue, and enables her to speed up.

She's no longer jogging on her wobbly legs. She's sprinting.

With trembling fingers, she grabs the doorknob and presses it down. The door opens, exposing the large engine room with its rusty, dust-covered appliances and the multitude of pipes and wires that wind along the surfaces of the walls on both sides.

And there she lies, curled up on the floor in the fetal position, a shackle attached to one foot.

Abby. Her beautiful, lovely—

A sound and a sensation interrupt her stream of thought.

The sound is brief, a quick *whoosh*, as if someone started blowing air across the top of an empty soda bottle and then stopped again right away.

The sensation, on the other hand, is longer lasting ... and twofold. At first, it's a short-lived but intense pain in her hamstring. Like an insect's sting. This is followed by a warmth spreading through her body, almost as if she has had a hot liquid injected into her veins.

She turns her head—no, she almost *sways* it, because it feels heavy, loose in some way—and looks down at herself.

There's ... something there? Where it felt like she got stung, there is a small, pink tuft of hair.

A new whooshing sound reaches her ears, but it doesn't trigger any pain this time. Apparently, though, it does for Chloe, who grabs her upper arm and grimaces.

On Chloe's arm sits another small tuft—and as she catches sight of it, Beth finally makes the connection.

She looks behind and sees him standing there, backlit at the end of the corridor.

The man with the ski mask.

The man with the tranquilizer gun.

She opens her mouth to warn Chloe, to scream at her to run and hide, but all that comes out are incoherent sounds.

Above her, the light starts flashing. No, not just the light. *Everything* is flashing. The world is flashing in and out.

Black.

The man approaches.

Black.

She is no longer in the corridor. She is on the floor in the engine room.

Black.

The man has a rope in his hand. He's using it to tie Chloe to one of the pipes. Beth tries to stop him, but she can't get over there, she can't get to him, she ...

Black.

She has a shackle on her foot.

December 19th

Abby

There is no hope left in Abby's heart—and what's worse, the same goes for her mom.

She tries to hide it by pulling her lips up in a smile every time Abby meets her gaze, but it's pure acting. A facade she puts up for the sake of her and Chloe.

It's the eyes that give it away. They're dull and lifeless, almost glassy. When the lips smile, her eyes still don't.

At first, Abby told herself that it was probably due to the tranquilizer not yet having worn off. But by now, many hours have passed since her mom and Chloe woke up. Maybe half a day.

Or half a night, she adds in her thoughts. *You don't really have any idea if it's day or night right now, do you?*

No, she doesn't. Her sense of time is completely screwed up. Guess that's just what happens when you're locked in a room with no windows for days ...

and when your head is repeatedly bashed against a concrete floor. That doesn't exactly help either.

With the exception of the tearful exchanges following in the wake of their reunion, they haven't spoken much either. Most of the time, all three of them just sit and stare blankly into the air.

To an outside observer, that might seem strange, given the circumstances, but Abby knows exactly what is causing their collective silence.

They're waiting. On him—and on the punishment that must come sooner or later.

And the wait is excruciating ... which he, undoubtedly, is well aware of.

By the time the door finally opens and the man with the goggles enters, Abby has already played out a myriad of variations of the moment in her head. She has seen him enter with a rifle in his hands, she has seen him enter with a knife, and she has even seen him enter dragging a new victim.

But the Christmas stocking he's holding in his hands as he makes his entrance is in many ways more frightening than all of these things.

For Abby knows what he usually puts in his Christmas stockings, and she immediately understands what it means when he places it on the floor in front of their mom and then continues over to the sliding door.

"Oh God, no," she hears her mom sob as he puts the key in the padlock that prevents trespassers from opening the sliding door and turns it. "Not in front of them. Not in front of my girls."

Chloe, who until now has been sitting still as a statue, staring at the man, widens her eyes and looks at Abby with a pleading expression.

Abby can't help her. Hell, Abby can't even form a coherent thought.

A shrill squeal rises from the rusty metal rail as the man pushes the sliding door aside. The door, which is really just a large wooden board hanging a bit above the floor, slides to the end of the rail and stops with a heavy clank, after which its bottom bumps against the wall a few times.

For a while, the man disappears into the room. When he returns, he has put on a rubber apron, and he once again has something in his hands.

In the right, a small branch cutter. In the left, a blowtorch.

With eerily calm movements—as if he were just an old man sorting cardboard boxes in a garage—he puts his tools in the pocket on the front of his apron and closes the sliding door again. He also locks it, even though all other people in the engine room are tied with rope or chained up.

After double-checking the padlock by pulling it, he shifts his attention back to his prisoners. He strolls—so laidback that it must be a deliberately theatrical act—over to their mom and squats in front of her.

And then he does something he hasn't done before. He speaks to her. Words that, despite them being whispered and muffled by the fabric of his mask, reach Abby's ears and send the icy fingers of terror crawling down her spine.

"Fight back and I'll continue with them afterward." These are the words he says—and while they're allowed to hang in the air for a moment, he frees the branch cutter from his apron. After that, he grabs their mom's wrist with his other hand and pulls so that her arm is stretched out.

"Are we clear?" he whispers, his voice little more than a heavy exhalation.

Their mom shakes and sobs uncontrollably yet somehow finds the strength to respond with a nod. And to suppress the impulse to resist, as he places his knee on her elbow to lock her arm in place.

"Let h-her go!" Abby stutters with a mouth that—like the rest of her body—is so paralyzed with horror that it feels like it's been sedated.

"No, Abby," her mom groans. "It's okay. Be quiet!"

It's *not* okay. Her mom's body is shuddering as if she were having an epileptic seizure. Her cheeks are wet, her hair soaked in sweat and sticking to her face. Threads of saliva and snot hang from her nose and her chin. It's anything but okay.

Now he lifts her hand and—*oh God, he's gonna do it*

—leads the cutter to it. He grabs her fingers and squeezes, leaving only one of them free, and ...

Look away! Look away, for God's sake!

Abby can't. Something keeps her gaze locked on her mom's pink little ring finger as it slides in between the blades of the cutter, and he presses.

The scream is deafening. Louder than anything she's ever heard coming out of her mom's mouth. Still, it's the other sound that causes Abby's skin to contract, making it feel as if she can't fit in it anymore.

It's the squelching, crunching sound of the skin, flesh, and eventually the bone giving in to the pressure. It's the sound of spit clicking against teeth when someone chews with their mouth open. A handful of jelly being squeezed between fingers. A bundle of raw spaghetti being broken in half.

Blood. A red fountain sending thin jets out on both sides of the branch cutter's blades as he twists it free again. Free of the bone that it has dug into.

A new crack, shards of glass beneath a boot heel, and it's free, but ... oh God, there's still a thin piece of skin connecting the severed finger to the rest of the hand. Now it's dangling below the other fingers. Swaying slightly from side to side. Like the dream-catcher beneath the rearview mirror in Bill's car.

Her mom is still screaming. Behind her, Chloe twists her head from side to side in panic and horror. That's all she can do since the rope is tight and keeps the rest of her body pressed against the pipe.

The man with the ski mask ignores them both and moves on to the next finger, still with completely calm movements.

The blades of the cutter dig into the flesh, her mom's legs jerk uncontrollably, it's squashing, it's crunching, and it's too much for Abby now. Her stomach contracts, sending a wave of bile up her throat. She vomits, expels the contents of her belly on the floor in front of her. A watery, greenish liquid with scattered lumps of partly dissolved sandwich bread.

And still, he doesn't care. He offers her no more than a fleeting glance before he puts the cutter back in the pocket of his apron, exchanging it for the blowtorch, and turns his attention back to the macabre ritual.

A faint hiss as he opens the gas supply. A click and an angry whoosh as he presses a button and turns the gas jet into a blue flame.

Abby shuts her eyes the moment the flame reaches her mother's hand, but to no avail. The scream—now mixed with a gurgling rasp from her mother's throat—tears through the darkness behind her eyelids, and it only takes seconds for the smell to hit her. A suffocating stench of burnt flesh stinging in her nostrils, leaving a vile, charred aftertaste on her tongue.

Once more, nausea spreads in her throat and contracts her stomach in a painful spasm.

In the hope of being able to suppress it, she grabs her own neck and opens her eyes.

And then, in an instant, both the nausea and the cramps are pushed into the background. Because on the opposite side of the engine room, the door is kicked open, whereafter a man comes tumbling in, roaring like a wild animal and with a thick branch raised above his head. A man she never thought she would see again.

Her dad.

It all happens so fast that Abby's eyes can barely keep up. One moment she sees her dad come crashing through the door with his improvised club raised above his head, and the next he is in the middle of the room, bringing it down over the man in the ski mask.

The branch hits the man on the side of the head with enough force to break one side of his goggles and send a handful of glass shards out across the concrete floor.

This is also where the still burning blowtorch ends up. It slips out of his hand and skids—dragging the little blue flame behind it like a tail of fire—across the surface of the floor, after which it disappears under the sliding door.

As her dad raises the branch and lands two more blows, Abby notices a worrying detail about him.

He is shaking, swaying from side to side. He is exhausted, perhaps on the verge of losing consciousness.

In contrast, the man on the floor has recovered from the initial disorientation, and he isn't just taking the blows anymore. He is parrying them with his legs and one arm.

Now, a second too late, Abby realizes why he is only using one hand to protect himself. The other has gone into the pocket of his apron.

"DAD, LOOK OUT! HE'S GOT A—"

That's all she has time for before the man's hand strikes like a cobra and buries the blades of the branch cutter in her dad's calf muscle.

His leg gives out beneath him, and he collapses sideways onto the floor next to the man, who doesn't hesitate to throw himself on top of him, wrapping his hands around his throat. Now he's sitting there, squeezing the life out of her dad, while the blue eyes behind the shattered lenses of his ski goggles are lit with madness and anger.

The branch is lying on the floor. A weapon Abby could use to even the odds if she could only reach it. But she can't. It's just out of her range. Her fingertips are no more than an inch away from it every time the shackle digs into her ankle and stops her.

She tries again, again, again, with no luck. All she achieves is tearing her foot to the point of bleeding, while her dad—for the second time—is dying right before her eyes.

His face is already discolored. Bluish-purple. Oh God, his eyes. They're bloodshot and bulging. As if they could pop out of their sockets at any moment and slide across the floor like the shards of glass and the blowtorch did.

A movement behind the two men catches her eye. It's her mom. She is sitting up now. She looks like a character in a horror movie; her hair is a mess, her left hand a misshapen lump of blood-smeared skin and burnt finger fragments, her face pale, and her eyes full of shock and horror.

Yet, there's something else in them as well. A determination that makes her look completely un-hinged.

Now, she stretches out her uninjured hand—but not toward the man with the ski mask like Abby would've expected. Instead, she reaches behind him, toward her dad's lower legs, which are kicking slower and slower now.

Suddenly, Abby understands, and an intoxicating wave of hope washes through her when she sees her mom grab the cutter, pull it out of his leg—and then jam it straight into the back of the man with the ski mask.

The pain forces the man to let go of his victim, and he half crawls, half rolls away while frantically grasping for the cutter that sits buried just below his left shoulder blade, out of his reach with about the same small distance as there was between the branch and Abby's fingers.

Apparently, he has realized that it's a lost cause,

because now he quits trying to get ahold of it and gets up instead.

For a moment he stands there, legs slightly spread, hands clenched, as if gathering strength for the final attack.

But then, out of nowhere, he starts chuckling behind the mask.

"What's so funny?" her mom hisses, but Abby already knows. For she caught a glimpse of his eyes behind the broken goggles, and she saw where his gaze was directed.

And as the man turns his back on them and, still chuckling, staggers out of the engine room, two things happen.

One is that Abby points to the opening between the floor and the sliding door to alert her parents to the small tendrils of smoke that are now rising.

The second is that the clock strikes midnight and a new day begins.

December 20th

Chloe

It hurts every time her dad pulls at the rope behind her back, but Chloe swallows the pain. She has to be strong now, because underneath it all—the shock, the horror, and the powerlessness—she recognizes that the fate of her family will be in her hands in a moment.

For something is burning behind the sliding door, and since her mom and Abby are still chained up, they can't run from the smoke and fire as it spreads.

Ironically, the key to their rescue is the thing that caused the fire.

The blowtorch. It slid under the door, and because it's locked, her dad can't get in there. What he can do, though, is pull the door slightly away from the wall at the bottom. The chain that the padlock is attached to allows him to do so.

And maybe—just maybe—the space in between will be big enough for Chloe to squeeze through.

"One more knot, and we'll be there, sweetie," he whispers behind her, his voice still raspy from when the man in the ski mask almost choked him to death.

"Okay," she replies through clenched teeth as he pulls at the rope and causes a burning sensation on her upper arm. "Just be quick."

He nods, pulls two more times—and suddenly all the pressure disappears from her body. For a moment, this almost causes her to collapse, but her dad catches her and turns her toward him.

"I know it's hard," he says. "But we don't have time to rest."

Chloe replies with a nod and then staggers over to the sliding door, where she crouches down.

Up close, the smoke is really unsettling. It looks like tiny, semi-transparent octopus tentacles groping their way across the front of the sliding door.

"Be careful, Chloe," her mom says.

"You can do it," her sister adds.

Chloe looks up to her left and sees her dad standing with his hands on the edge of the large board that makes up the door. He asks with a nod, and she answers with a nod. Next, he pulls out the door until the chain with the padlock is fully extended.

Chloe peeks through the opening—and gasps.

The room isn't very big. It looks like a workshop similar to the one her granddad had in his garage when he was still alive. There is a table along the wall and a pegboard with various tools. In particular, there is a wide array of knives hanging on it, but she doesn't want to think too much about that.

To the left of the worktable is a stand with a curtain, like the ones used for dividing patient rooms in hospitals. It's this curtain that has caught fire, which makes sense, given that the blowtorch is lying on the floor just below it.

Her gaze slides upward, but where she had expected to find the ceiling, there's nothing but a thick blanket of smoke that takes on a menacing orange glow whenever the flames flare up.

All of a sudden, she's no longer sure she can bring herself to crawl in there.

"I can't keep holding it," her dad says behind her.

"Sorry, I'm gonna do it now," she says—and to her own surprise, that's exactly what she does. She edges through the gap.

The blend of smoke and heat is far worse than she expected. Her lungs burn when she breathes, and her eyes feel like they're going to dry out if she doesn't blink all the time.

She crawls on all fours across the floor. It's the only cool thing—the surface of the concrete floor. Everything else is trying to roast her alive.

"You're almost there," her dad reassures her. She looks back and sees him peeking through the crack. He looks hopeful and terrified at the same time.

He is right, though. She is almost there. The blow-torch is less than four feet away from her now. All she has to do is reach out her arm and—

Somewhere above her, three small pops sound, like when you burst bubbles on bubble wrap.

It's the curtain on the room divider. Or rather, it's the small plastic hooks at the top keeping it attached to the pole that are starting to give in to the heat. The inevitable consequence is that the burning curtain falls down. This happens in two steps. First, it lets go of one side, which causes it to swing backward, right before melting off the remaining hooks so it falls all the way down.

The good news is that it lands behind the blow-torch and not on top of it. The bad news is that it lands on something else.

It lands on the stomach of Bill's lifeless body.

His eyes. Chloe can't force her gaze away from them. And she can't get her body to move either.

Marbles. Grayish-blue matte marbles filled with fog and emptiness.

Their old neighbor, Mrs. Thompson, had a dog. A chubby French bulldog. It had cataracts, and in the last two years before it died, it went completely blind.

It had the same eyes—and although she never admitted it to Mrs. Thompson, those eyes scared the life out of Chloe every time the dog turned its head in her direction.

Bill has those eyes now.

He's dead, she says to herself. *He can't do anything to you.*

That's great, but his murky, lifeless eyes are still staring at her, and the bloody lump of flesh that was once his left hand lies on the floor less than three feet away from the blowtorch. And she knows—without a trace of doubt—that she would die if that hand were to move while she's reaching for the blowtorch.

She would, quite simply, die of fear.

"Chloe, sweetie?"

That's all her dad says, but it's also enough to remind her of the predicament they're in. And her job in it.

She takes one final breath of smoky air and reaches out her hand toward the blowtorch.

And yes, there was a split second where she considered doing it with her eyes closed so she didn't have to look in the direction of Bill's body.

But it's too risky. On the one hand, the blowtorch is still burning, so she could scorch herself, and on the other hand, there is the even worse risk that she could miss it so that her fingertips would meet Bill's lifeless body instead of the blowtorch.

Carefully, so she doesn't get too close to its jet, she grabs the blowtorch—and at that very instant, one of the flames from the burning curtain reaches Bill's hair.

It flares up a second, then melts and settles on his head like a thick, tarry mass.

This nightmare image is the last Chloe sees before she turns around and crawls back toward the sliding door, trembling and gasping with horror.

"You're so freaking cool, sis," Abby exclaims as Chloe comes out through the narrow opening and hands the blowtorch to her dad, who immediately brings it over to Abby's ankle shackle and starts to cut the chain.

Meanwhile, Chloe crawls away from the sliding door—away from the smoke and heat—and sits with her back resting against one of the pipes.

"Are you okay?" her mom asks.

Chloe tries to answer but can't. She doesn't have enough air to form words, and her lungs refuse to take any in. She gasps for air, getting nothing but the bitter taste of coal on her tongue and tightness in her chest. It feels as though some invisible hands have reached in, grabbed her lungs, and are squeezing them.

"What's wrong?" one of the others asks. She doesn't know who as the voice sounds distant and muffled—and the floor has started to sway, so she has a hard time focusing on their faces.

In a foggy state of shock and panic, she grabs her chest, her neck.

"You can't breathe?" the floaty dream voice asks from the bottom of a deep well, and Chloe responds by shaking her head and hitting herself on the chest.

"Oh God! Help her, Adam!"

That one was her mom. Chloe is sure of that, even though the well is constantly getting deeper and the voices are moving further away.

Just like the engine room. It's also slowly evaporating around her, dissolving and getting replaced by darkness.

Under the murky marble eyes, Bill's chapped lips pull up into a smile. He reaches out his hands, the crooked lumps of flesh that's left of them, and grabs Chloe. Shakes her.

She wakes up with a scream, and he still has her. He clutches her, squeezes her, presses her against his cold, dead body, he—

No. Not Bill. Her dad. He's ... carrying her, just like when she was little. It sounds like it's killing him, and she can feel him tilting to the sides as if he's struggling to keep his balance.

She blinks a couple of times, and slowly, the blurred filter covering everything comes off.

Hazy geometric shapes become doors, notice boards, and office furniture. They're still in the abandoned radio station but no longer in the engine room. Her mom and sister have also been freed from their chains. They're walking a few yards further back. They have their arms around each other's backs, and they both look like it causes them pain every time they move their feet.

"Hey, sweetie," her dad sighs. "How are you?"

"Okay, I think. My head hurts. What happened?"

"You passed out. We think it was because of the smoke in there. But we're on our way out now. It'll be good for you to get some fresh air."

Chloe blinks her eyes again. He says so many words, and she has a hard time keeping up. It makes her headache worse.

Something red flicks by in the corner of her eye, and she instinctively grabs ahold of her dad's coat.

"Dad, stop! Wait!"

"We can't, sweetie. It's still burning back there, and we don't know if there are old gas lines and stuff like that in the building that could explode."

"But ... but you *have to* stop. There's food in there."

That was the magic word. He stops and looks at her.

"What do you mean?"

"The door behind the red cabinet over there, it leads into a kitchen. That's where he hides the food."

"How do you ... never mind. You're sure about it?"

"Totally."

Her dad hesitates for a moment and then looks at her mom, who nods.

"If we are going out there again, bringing food and water isn't a bad idea," she says.

"Fair enough, but we have to be quick about it." He looks at Chloe again. "Do you think you can walk, sweetie? I don't think I'm able to carry you much longer."

Chloe replies with a nod. That's all she's capable of because her throat is starting to burn again and her lungs feel like they've been put in a blacksmith's vise.

December 21st

❦

Adam

Adam should feel grateful. Against all odds, he found his family again and saved them from the torture chamber of a murderous maniac. He should be patting himself on the back, saying *well done, buddy*.

There's just one problem. A minor detail with colossal implications. He saved them from one version of hell but dumped them straight down into another.

And it *is* hell out here in the snowy mountains. Adam had several days to think about this when he wandered around in it alone. A blinding white, bitterly cold hell that constantly wears on your body and soul. One example of this is the gunshot wound in his thigh, which is starting to throb again. He had hoped that the adrenaline rush that kept him going inside the radio station would last and lead to a rapid healing, but unfortunately that wasn't the case. The pain is back at full strength.

Searching for spots with mobile coverage has also become futile, since his own phone was in his pocket and was broken when he fell into the canyon—and the three they have left are completely dead. Either the batteries are drained, or they have been damaged by lying in the damp backpack. Whatever the reason, they refuse to turn on.

To be fair, Adam does have one positive thing to cling to. They haven't seen or heard anything from the man in the ski mask since he left them in the burning building. But considering that two of them were still chained up when he fled, he probably assumes that the fire took care of them. Nevertheless, they still chose to head directly for the woods when they got out, hoping it would better their chances of avoiding him.

Somewhere behind Adam, there is a strained, croaking cough. He doesn't need to look to know who it's coming from.

"Don't forget to let me know if you need a break, sweetie."

"It's okay, Dad. My throat just hurts again. But it's getting better, I think."

Hardly has Chloe said those words before Beth appears next to Adam.

"She's lying. You know that, right? It's only gotten worse since yesterday, and she's coughing all the time now."

Adam sighs and nods.

"I know. I just don't know what to do about it. We

have to just keep going and pray that we find a road or something soon."

A pause, then Beth nods and strokes his arm with her unscathed hand. The other is bound in an improvised bandage made from a tea towel they found in the radio station's kitchen—and that hand practically hasn't left the pocket of her coat in the past twenty-four hours.

"I'm sorry," she says. "I know you're doing what you can."

"You don't have to apologize."

Another pause, then Beth swallows uneasily and touches his arm again.

"Yes, I do, Adam," she says. "I do owe you an apology. When I think about what you must have gone through to get back to us, I ..."

She finishes the sentence with a shudder as the image sends a cold chill down her spine.

Adam opens his mouth but can't think of anything relevant to say, so he closes it again and gives her a delicate smile instead.

Beth also smiles ... but she has tears in her eyes.

"I haven't been fair to you," she says. "I blamed you for so many things. Not just about the vacation. Before that too. And when I saw you falling over the edge, I ... I thought ..."

Adam takes her hand in his and gives it a squeeze while shaking his head.

"We are both to blame, Beth. It's not like I deserve a

medal for my presence in our relationship in the past year or so, you know?"

Beth shrugs and lets her gaze fall to the ground.

"But none of that matters anymore," Adam continues. "Because we're gonna make it."

She hesitates for a long time, and when she finally meets his gaze again, she looks uncertain. Almost scared.

"Are you sure?"

"With all the shit I've been through to get you guys back?" Adam says and smiles. "You bet your sweet little ass I am. We're gonna make it. And I'm not just talking about the hike down from the mountain. Alright?"

Beth wipes her cheeks with her sleeve and nods at him. Her eyes are still wet, but the expression in them is solemn. It tells him that she trusts him when he says that they'll make it.

And for the first time since returning to this white version of hell, there is also a part of him that believes in it.

"Here, press this against your forehead, sweetie."

Chloe looks at the snowball in Adam's hand as if it were a bowlful of deep-fried spider legs.

"For the fever," he elaborates.

Chloe still doesn't look convinced, but at least she accepts the snowball and does what he asks her to.

It's not that he doesn't understand her skepticism. Trying to lower her body temperature seems counter-intuitive, considering that all four of them are already chattering their teeth. But damn it, he is her *dad*. He has to do something.

"Do you want some more to eat?" Beth asks. She is sitting with Abby by a small fire that Adam made when they set up camp for the night.

"No thanks."

"Chloe?"

"Nah, I'm not hungry."

For a moment, Beth looks as if she is going to insist that the patient eat, but then she changes her mind and puts the sandwich back in her bag.

Whether or not to light a fire was no easy decision, but they ended up agreeing that it was worth the risk. Mainly because they are surrounded by trees, so it won't be visible from very far away.

"Do you think we'll get down tomorrow?" Chloe asks.

Adam hesitates for a long time before answering because his first impulse—the comforting lie—doesn't feel worth it anymore. It might have a week ago, but he's not the only one who's been through hell, and Chloe isn't the girl she was a week ago. You only need to take a single glance at the eyes above her fever-flushed cheeks to know that.

"Honestly," he says, "I don't know. I hope and believe that we'll get down safely. But whether it's going to be tomorrow ..."

He ends the sentence with a shrug of the shoulders and turns his gaze to the sky, where darkness is settling over the mountains like a black cloak, suffocating the last remnants of daylight.

Chloe coughs again. A faint, croaking sound that tears the silence and makes all the remaining members of the family glance in her direction with concern in their eyes.

"I think it would be a good idea if you rested a bit," Adam says, stroking a hand over her hair.

"It's okay. I'm not tired."

That has to be the lie of the century. Her gaze is drowsy, her voice hollow and muddy.

Adam looks at her, studying the expression in her eyes.

"If you're afraid he's going to come back, you should know that—"

"It's not that," Chloe says, turning her face away.

"Then what?"

"It's just ... I don't want to sleep if I get nightmares."

She pauses, presumably considering whether she wants to elaborate or not, and Adam lets her do so.

"It's Bill," she finally says. "He was in the room when I got the blowtorch. He was, um ... he was dead, Dad, and he caught fire when the curtain fell down."

The words hit Adam like a blow to the stomach,

rendering him unable to speak. And when he gets his voice back, he has no idea what to say.

"Christ, sweetie. I'm so sorry you had to go through that. If I had known ..."

He never finishes the sentence, partly because he is interrupted when Chloe suddenly throws herself into his arms, and partly because he can't honestly say that it would have made a difference if he had known that Bill was in there. The blowtorch was the only solution to the ankle shackles, and Chloe was the only one able to get ahold of it.

Still, the thought of how scared she must have been is agonizing.

He pulls her closer and feels her forehead against his neck. It's scorching hot. There's no doubt that the fever is bad. He can only pray that it won't get worse during the night.

Because with what she has just told him, it isn't difficult to imagine what her subconscious would torment her with if the fever should induce hallucinations.

December 22nd

∽

Beth

A short distance from the night's campsite is a fallen tree, the gnarled roots of which have been torn up, so they now hang like a natural canopy over the large hole they have left in the ground.

Beneath that canopy, Beth sits. She came here under the pretense of having to pee, but that wasn't the real reason.

Beth came here to be alone. She came here to cry.

And that's exactly what she does. She sits on the ground, staring at her hand—and at the empty spaces where two of her fingers used to be—while tears stream down her cheeks.

She doesn't know how long she's been sitting here, but the sky was orange-red when she sat down, and it's light blue now. The day has begun.

Another day.

She closes her eyes and swallows the pain as she bends her fingers one at a time. They're there. She can feel them all, their tips touching the palm of her hand.

She opens her eyes—and is bitterly corrected. The two burnt pieces will never ever again be able to reach the palm of her hand, no matter how hard they try.

That thought brings new tears to her cheeks, but that's okay. That's what she came here for. Venting. Letting it all out from the start, so she, hopefully, is able to make it through the rest of the day without breaking down in front of the girls. Heaven knows they have enough to deal with as it is. Especially Chloe. She has been coughing most of the night, and the few times she managed to fall asleep, it didn't take long before she woke up again. Screaming.

Without really knowing why, Beth raises her hand up to her nose and smells the burnt bits. It smells like barbecue meat ... and the worst part is that it makes her stomach rumble. How sick is that?

Something crunches behind her, causing her to jolt and look behind.

"I'm sorry. I didn't mean to scare you."

"It's okay, Abby. I was just caught up in my own little world."

"Yeah, I see that. Does it hurt a lot?"

Only now does Beth realize that she is still sitting with her hand in front of her face, and she hurries to put it in her pocket.

"Nah, it's not so bad," she lies. "It's mostly if I bump into something."

"Oh yeah, I can imagine that," Abby says with what should be a smile but doesn't quite get all the way there.

"There's room for one more," Beth says, patting the ground next to her.

Abby shrugs her shoulders and then sits down.

For a while, none of them say anything. They just sit next to each other, mother and daughter, with their gazes directed inward. Then Abby suddenly clears her throat and says:

"I'm so beat, Mom. I'm not sure I can keep on doing this."

"I know, sweetie. So am I, but we've got to—"

"And I'm worried about Chloe. She looks so sick, and she is coughing all the time now."

"Your sister is strong. She'll be alright."

Out of the corner of her eye, she can sense that Abby is seeking eye contact with her—perhaps to test to what extent her mom actually believes her own words—but it's more than Beth can give her right now.

For a moment, she's afraid that Abby will insist. That she'll demand that she look at her and repeat it, but when Abby opens her mouth, something completely different comes out. Nevertheless, there is still a touch of disappointment in her voice as she says:

"I, um ... came to tell you that the others are ready to go."

"Oh, sure, of course," Beth says. "Then we'd better get back to them."

Eight excruciating hours later, the miracle occurs. Beth spots a road. It cuts through the landscape at the foot of the mountainside they're walking on. It isn't very large and probably won't lead to Rome ... but it has to lead to a town somewhere.

To help.

"ADAM!" she shouts in a quivering voice. "ADAM, GET OVER HERE. NOW!"

She knows he is walking with the girls a good distance behind and that he is on the verge of collapsing from exhaustion. But she needs him to see it. She needs him to confirm that the road is really there.

"WHAT'S GOING ON?"

She turns around and sees him staggering out from a cluster of trees on the slope.

"A r-road," she sobs. "There's a road down there."

"What? I can't understand what you're saying, hon."

Instead of repeating the words, Beth raises her unhurt hand and points.

Adam follows the invisible line from her fingertip and down the slope. And once his gaze finds its destination, he emits a sound that is a strange cross between laughing and crying.

Five more steps bring him all the way over to Beth, and as he reaches her, he grabs her hand and pulls her to him.

"I told you," he half whispers, half sobs. "Didn't I tell you we'd make it?"

"You did, hon," she replies—and for the first time since leaving the cabin, she hears herself laugh.

Behind Adam's back, the girls emerge between the tree trunks. They're walking hand in hand. They've done that most of the day.

"What's going on?" Abby asks—and once again, Beth is forced to answer by pointing because her vocal cords won't obey.

"Is that a *road?*" Abby exclaims, and without waiting for an answer, she grabs her sister by the shoulders. "There's a road, Chloe. Oh God, we're going home!"

Chloe nods, takes a deep breath—and lets it out again in a worrying fit of coughing. She smiles, though, despite the pain.

"How far do you think it is?" Beth asks. "Can we make it down there before it gets dark?"

"Down to the road, yes," Adam replies. "But we don't know how far it is from there to the nearest town."

Beth looks at the road, then at the white mountain landscape behind them, and finally back at the road again. And then she makes her decision.

"I don't know about you guys," she says, "but I've slept out here for the last time. Even if I have to trudge along that road all night, I'm not stopping until we've found help. If nothing else, a car has to come by at some point, right?"

She lets her gaze travel across the faces of the others until she has received a nod from each of them. Then she turns around and resumes their grueling hike.

This time with the goal clearly in sight.

December 23rd

❦

Abby

Beneath the thick layer of snow and with the bluish glow from the low-hanging moon as their only light source, the road is nearly invisible. Thankfully, there is a faint tire track from a vehicle that has made its way through. They've used it as a guide most of the night, and apart from a stretch where the drifting snow had completely erased it, it has kept them on the right path.

Now, however, they've found something else to navigate by. It's hovering out there on the horizon like a lonely lighthouse in the night. A faint, flickering light from an old neon sign.

"I'm telling you it is," Abby hears her mom say somewhere behind her. "It's the same."

"I'm still not convinced," her dad replies.

They're debating whether the neon sign belongs to the gas station they stopped at on the way up to the cabin. The place where they met with Bill.

That seems like a lifetime ago. In some way, one could argue that it is. At least, Abby's life will never be the same again. That's for sure.

"You really can't see that it's the same sign?" her mom continues. "Look at the last letter. It's tilted. Just like it was ..."

She keeps going, but Abby isn't really listening anymore. To be honest, she couldn't care less whether it's the same gas station or not. As long as there's a phone, she is content. She suspects that her mom and dad feel the same way but are just trying to fend off the fatigue by keeping the conversation going.

That thought instinctively makes her glance over at her little sister. Because Chloe is taking the exact opposite approach. She doesn't speak at all. She just staggers along with her eyes fixed on the ground, and the only sounds escaping her mouth are heavy, wheezing coughs and a stubborn *no thanks* when one of her parents offer to carry her.

Abby moves over beside her, wraps an arm around her back, and whispers:

"How are you holding up, sis?"

Chloe lifts her head and looks at her through a little white cloud that her breath makes in the cold air.

"Mom and Dad think I've got smoke poisoning. I heard them whispering about it earlier."

She says the words without emotion as if it were just a dry fact she happened to stumble upon in an old encyclopedia. Either she doesn't fully grasp the gravity of it, or she's too deep in the fever bubble to express her feelings properly. Could be a bit of both.

"Yeah, I heard it too," Abby says. "But they also said they weren't sure. So maybe we should just wait and see what the doctors say today."

It takes a moment—a long moment—before the comprehension dawns in Chloe's eyes.

"Today?" she says and smiles.

"Yup, we're past midnight, aren't we? And it won't be long before we're at the gas station."

As if to prove her claim, Abby nods in the direction of the neon sign still blinking in the darkness ahead.

"Today," Chloe repeats in a voice so subdued that it's probably just a thought she's muttering to herself. "We're going home *today*."

Abby could correct her and point out that Chloe will probably have to spend at least a couple of days in a hospital before she can go *home*.

Abby doesn't say anything, though. She simply strokes her hand over her sister's back and smiles at her.

Their mom was right. The old flickering neon sign indeed belongs to the gas station where they met with Bill. Even Abby can see that now—and she had her eyes locked on the screen of her phone most of the time while they were parked here.

This time, it's different. This time, she thoroughly studies the old, rundown gas station out here in the middle of nowhere. She looks at the two worn gas pumps, whose housings are so rusty that the numbers on them are almost unreadable, and she looks at the roof above them, where the snow has accumulated in heavy drifts. But above all else, she looks at the dark windows in the store's facade. Because in there is where they'll find the phone that will be their salvation.

"The store is closed," Chloe says as they enter the parking lot. "Does that mean we have to wait until morning?"

"We aren't waiting for anything," their dad replies, after which he walks straight to the front of the store and grabs a propane canister from a pallet standing next to the entrance.

"Isn't that dangerous?" Abby asks when she sees him lift the gas canister, preparing to hammer its bottom against the glass doors at the entrance. "I mean, can't it, like ... explode or something?"

Her dad looks at her for a moment, perplexed. Then he realizes what she means, and he sends her a reassuring smile.

"They only blow up that easily in movies, sweetie. For this to explode, I'd have to open the valve first. Besides, I'd need to make a spark, at least."

Abby nods but still doesn't feel entirely safe when

he swings the canister back over one shoulder and then thrusts it forward.

A loud clang. A modest fracture.

He sighs, takes a deep breath, and then tries again.

This time, the fracture grows and spreads, forming an intricate pattern resembling the root network of a large tree ... but there is still no opening.

"Fuck," her dad groans, grimacing as he grabs his thigh. "It's harder than I thought."

"Do you want me to try?" their mom asks.

"I just need to catch my breath," he replies, glaring at the sliding door with his eyes squinted as if to say *we aren't done with each other yet, pal.*

Two deep breaths later, he raises the gas canister again and sends it forward.

A sharp, quivering sound travels through the glass, and fresh cracks branch out in all directions. And then, in a sudden explosion, the door gives way. Shards of glass rain down, some large and jagged, others tiny like glittering dust.

Her dad edges his way through the opening, glances from side to side, and then nods to the others.

Abby is next to step into the darkness of the store. And it really *is* dark, much darker than she expected it to be. She can only make out the edges of the nearest shelves. The rest is reduced to dark outlines.

It's also quiet. Apart from the sound of crunching glass beneath the soles of their shoes, there's only a soft hum from a cooler and a muffled, monotonous ticking from a clock she can't see.

"Can't you turn on the light?" her mom asks as she enters.

"If I could, I would," her dad replies. "I just haven't found a switch yet ... Abby?"

"Nope, me neither. Could it be in a back room, maybe?"

"I guess, but it's ... oh, wait a sec."

He doesn't say anything else, and Abby is about to ask what they're waiting for when the answer comes in the form of a small, orange flame. Behind it, her dad's face glows in the dim light.

"I put the lighter in my pocket after making the fire yesterday," he says, shrugging. "I forgot. Sorry."

It's not the world's brightest lighting, but it's far better than nothing, and it allows them to move around the store without bumping into the shelves all the time.

The counter is at the opposite end of the store. That has to be the best place to look for a phone.

Her dad must have had a similar thought. At least, he is also heading straight toward the counter.

"Let me know if you find a light switch," he says as he rounds the corner and moves behind the counter. On the wall behind him, a poster is illuminated, showing a man behind the wheel of a car. He's yawning, his half-open, bloodshot eyes staring ahead, and beneath him the text reads:

ON THE ROAD FOR A LONG TIME?

NO WORRIES, WE'VE GOT YOU COVERED!

FRESHLY BREWED COFFEE, ONLY $1.99!

The photo brings a smile to Abby's face. It's not that she finds it especially original or funny; she can, however, appreciate the irony of the man in the picture looking significantly fresher than every single member of their little family right now.

"This can't be right!" her dad groans behind the counter. He sounds frustrated, almost angry.

"What's the matter, Adam?"

"No phone," he replies through clenched teeth. "No phone and no light switch. How the hell can there not be a phone?"

Three things happen immediately after those words. The first is that the old fluorescent tube in the ceiling flashes a few times and then the store is lit in a dusty, blue-white light. The next is the sound of two clanks in rapid succession—the unmistakable sound of a shotgun being loaded. The last thing is that her dad's question is answered by a deep male voice coming from the store's entrance.

"There's no landline in the store because I'm the only one running the station, and I always keep the company phone in my pocket," says the voice. "Now would you be so kind as to tell me what the hell you're doing in here ... before I sprinkle some pellets in your backsides?"

～

The elderly gentleman in the doorway doesn't look like a man you'd want to piss off. The gray eyes in his weathered face are cold and steely, as if they have seen everything life has to offer and then some. His hands are wrinkled and speckled with liver spots, but they're eerily calm. There is no doubt that the pellets will hit exactly where he wants them to, should he decide to pull the trigger of the shotgun.

"I'm still waiting," he says, fixing his gaze on her dad. Nonetheless, it's her mom who speaks first.

"We ... aren't normally like this," she says. "We would never do something like this if it wasn't a matter of life or death."

Almost as a supplement to her words, Chloe breaks out in a coughing fit. She tries to muffle it with her sleeve, but it's still loud in the quiet store.

"You don't remember me at all?" her dad suddenly asks. "We talked on the day we arrived. We were going to rent Bill Tavern's cabin, and you, um ... you told me how far out in the country it was."

The old man squints his eyes, and for a moment, Abby thinks there's a trace of recognition in them, but then he shakes his head.

"You broke my door."

"We're gonna replace it," her mom says, holding up a hand in front of her. "I promise. But right now, we really, *really* need to borrow your phone."

"Oh, that's priceless. If you think—"

"Look at us!" her dad interrupts, his voice shrill and

full of despair. "Please, just look at us for a second. We've been through hell, okay? My family has been held captive, I've been shot, and we were very close to dying in a fire. So, won't you please just take a moment and look at us?"

For a split second, Abby is convinced that her dad's outburst will be the last drop in an already full cup and that the man will send a cascade of pellets in their direction. Luckily, that doesn't happen. The old man does what her dad asks him to. He looks at them, lets his gaze wander from one to the other—and when it reaches her mom's hand, the expression on his face changes. The hardness is replaced by shock.

"Who did that?" he asks in a voice that suddenly seems hollow and empty.

"We don't know," Abby replies. "He was wearing a mask."

"We really are sorry that we broke your door," her dad says. "But we needed to get to a phone so we could call for help, and it just couldn't wait."

The gas station attendant rubs the back of his neck and looks up toward the ceiling for a moment as if to say *what the hell is this?* Then he reaches into the pocket of his coat. When his hand reappears, he's holding a cell phone, which he hands to her mom.

"You have no idea how grateful we are for this," she says. "You just saved our lives."

The older gentleman wrinkles his nose and nods his head slightly but says nothing.

Abby watches her mom press the *Home* button and wake the phone to life. She also sees her tap the screen a few times and then raise it to her ear—and the second she sees the bluish glow from the screen light up her mom's cheek, it hits her for real.

They're getting rescued. The nightmare is over.

She gets about three seconds with that thought before a flash of light out in the parking lot, accompanied by a loud bang, causes the entire house of cards to collapse and reopens the gate to Hell.

Not only does Abby see it happen. She sees it happen *slowly* because her brain somehow decelerates time, making her experience the event as if it were a slow-motion replay of a goal in a sports game.

And slow-motion means details. Things like the old gas attendant's head tilting sideways with a crack when the bullet hits his temple and penetrates the skin. Things like blood and small lumps of brain matter that squirt out on the other side when the bullet exits. Things like his body collapsing on the floor in a position that shouldn't be physically possible.

Abby has never screamed inside of her mind before, but she does now.

Behind the gas attendant's collapsed body, another man now appears in the doorway. The goggles are gone, but he's still wearing the white ski mask.

It's him. Their nightmare.

Shards of glass snap under his boots as he steps inside and sweeps his revolver in a slow semicircle through the air so that its barrel points at all the other members of the family before finally stopping on her dad.

"You're a tough bunch," he hisses through the fabric of the mask. "I'll give you that much. How'd you get them out of the chains?"

Her dad doesn't say anything. Neither do any of the others.

"It doesn't matter," the man says, motioning for them to step outside by tilting the revolver in the direction of the broken door. "You'll have plenty of time to tell me about it when we get back."

Back. It takes a second for the word to really sink in with Abby, but when it does, panic creeps over her spine like a thorny vine.

"Nope," the man says as her dad makes a move to leave his spot behind the counter and step out into the store. "You stay right there until the others are outside."

He nods toward her mom and Chloe, who are standing by a shelf on the left side of the store.

"You two first, then Abby. Daddy last."

Honestly, it shouldn't come as a shock to Abby that the maniac knows her name. He must've heard Chloe say it several times when they were trapped in the engine room. Nevertheless, the sound of it—in *his* mouth—chills her to the bone.

"Come on, get a move on," he says, threatening her mom with the gun. "Go out and wait by the pumps. And don't get any clever ideas."

Once Chloe and her mom are outside, he turns to Abby.

"You're up."

Abby nods and turns her gaze downward to avoid eye contact with him as she walks by.

That's part of the reason. Another part is that looking down allows her to scan the floor tiles without him noticing.

She's almost outside when she spots it. It's lying in the shadows beneath one of the shelves on the left side of the broken glass door.

The gas station clerk's shotgun.

She stares at it hesitantly, her pulse rising in her temples until it drowns out all other sounds.

She doesn't want to, but she doesn't have a choice. So, she throws herself down on her knees and reaches for it.

Abby has underestimated her opponent. She realizes this immediately when she turns around after picking up the shotgun from the floor. A microsecond from pulling the trigger past the critical point, she stops herself.

He has her dad. One arm is locked around his neck,

the other holds the muzzle of the revolver pressed against his temple.

"Let him g-go," Abby stammers, bitterly aware that she's not the one with the upper hand.

He knows it too. The mask hides his mouth, but she can sense the smile in his eyes.

"Just give up," he says. "Hasn't this gone far enough?"

While speaking, he steps toward her, still holding her dad in front of him like a human shield—and for every step he takes in her direction, Abby takes one back. That way, he slowly drives her out of the store, and he doesn't stop until she's all the way out under the canopy and he's standing in the entrance.

"Let him go," she repeats, but her voice is as pathetic and feeble as the threat it's trying to convey. "Let him go, or I'll shoot!"

"Is that so? Guess you must be a good shot, then. It's not easy hitting a target precisely with a shotgun like that one."

"Abby," her dad says calmly, but she immediately shakes her head. She knows what he's going to say. He wants her to pull the trigger. He'll say it's the only solution. That she shouldn't worry about him. That she has to save her mom and her little sister.

"ABBY, LOOK AT ME!" he suddenly shouts—and this time her gaze instinctively moves up to his face.

"No, Dad," she sobs. "I don't want to—"

"Abby, you need to put it down," her dad interrupts,

holding one hand up in front of him. "He's right. It's a shotgun. You'll never hit him without hitting me too."

For a moment, Abby is unable to do anything but stare at him in disbelief as her brain shifts into overdrive, trying to make sense of the words ... and the betrayal within them.

Then she sees it. The slight movement he makes with the hand he *isn't* holding up in front of him. He opens and closes it again, giving her a brief glimpse of the small metal object he is holding in it.

And when she subsequently sees his gaze wander down to the pallet of propane canisters standing along the wall next to the store's entrance—less than three feet from him—the pieces fall into place.

"I'm serious, sweetie," he continues. "We can't win this one. So now, I want you to take two deep breaths, and then you put the shotgun down on the ground, okay?"

Without breaking eye contact with her dad, Abby bites her lip and responds with a heavy nod. After that, she takes her two deep breaths ... but instead of putting the shotgun away, she aims its barrel at the gas canisters.

This unexpected turn of events triggers a moment's confusion in the man in the ski mask and thus provides an opening for her dad, who slams his elbow into his stomach. He does this at the exact moment Abby pulls the trigger. And while the man in the ski mask tumbles backward through the doorway, her dad flicks the lighter and tosses it toward the canisters, now hissing like a bunch of angry snakes.

The silhouette of her dad being thrown mercilessly across the ground as a blanket of fire rolls over the underside of the canopy is the last thing Abby registers before the same invisible force pushes her backward.

Abby blinks her way out of the dark and finds herself lying on her back. Her ears are ringing, and the world around her is a blurry mess of movements and colors.

Her back is cold, wet. It's snow she is lying on. She ... isn't underneath the canopy anymore? She has ended up out in the middle of the parking lot. She raises her head and tries to focus, but her vision drifts.

Out of the corner of her eye, she picks up a movement. Legs. Feet. Someone is coming toward her.

Hardly has she finished this thought before that someone grabs her arm and pulls. She protests, says that it hurts, but is stunned when she realizes that she can't even hear her own voice.

She looks up and meets her mom's eyes, wide open and full of desperation. Her mouth is also open, and her lips form words, but it's like listening through water, and all Abby can do is shake her head.

Behind her mom, Chloe appears. She grabs the other arm, and this time, Abby doesn't resist. She lets them drag her away. Away from the burning store, away from the canopy, away from ...

Panic spreads in her like wildfire as it all comes back to her. Not only the memory of what happened, but also her senses. The noise from the crackling fire, the smell of smoke and burnt metal. The image of her dad being flung through the air like a rag doll.

"Where is he?" she asks. "Is Dad okay?"

"We pulled him away from the fire," her mom groans. "He ... got burned, but he is going to make it."

"And what about ... him?" Abby says, glancing toward the burning gas station.

"He's gone," her mom says—and after a moment's hesitation, she adds, "The fire got ahold of him."

Abby nods and closes her eyes for what feels like a second. It must have been much longer, though, because when she opens them again, she is lying on the other side of the road, and her mom isn't dragging her anymore. She is sitting on the ground with one arm around Chloe, who alternately coughs and gasps for breath. The other arm rests on her own thigh, and in its hand—supported by the three fingers left on it—is the gas station attendant's mobile phone.

Its screen is glowing with a delicate, light blue color, and across it is a notification text that dries up Abby's throat and brings tears of relief to her eyes.

911—CALL ENDED.

December 24th

❦

Chloe

Chloe wakes up to the sound of a soft, rhythmic whooshing, which to an outsider might resemble the sound of waves rolling onto a shore. It's not, though. The sound is coming from the oxygen machine next to her hospital bed. She doesn't need to open her eyes to know that. They connected her to the machine yesterday, and she has slept with the mask on all night.

Slowly, she opens her eyes—and to her surprise, she spots something that wasn't there when she fell asleep last night. It's a pine branch decorated with a small red bow. It's hanging from the ceiling, three feet above her bed.

She turns her head and looks around the room. There are Christmas decorations here and there; a red garland above the door, a couple of elves on the bed-side table. Clearly, someone has tried to bring a bit of

Christmas cheer into the otherwise cold and sterile space.

And why not? After all, today is the twenty-fourth of December. Christmas Eve ... which she'll be spending in a hospital bed, wearing an oxygen mask that is a little too tight for her taste.

A rattling sound from the doorway catches her attention. It's a cleaning lady, entering with a cart.

"Oh, you're awake?" she says as she catches sight of Chloe. "Your sister will be happy to hear that. She's been sitting in here most of the night."

"Is she here?" Chloe asks, but her voice is barely audible behind the plastic of the oxygen mask, and the cleaning lady doesn't seem to understand a single word. Nevertheless, she ends up answering the question anyway as she parks the cart and says:

"You know what? I actually think I passed your sister just a moment ago by the common room. Would you like me to go get her for you?"

Chloe nods and pulls down her mask a little so she can speak.

"I'd like that very much. Thank you."

"Oh, please," the cleaning lady replies, winking at her. "It's Christmas, isn't it?"

Chloe smiles and glances up at the branch with the red bow. Something tells her that this cleaning lady might just be the one behind it.

Abby can't have been very far away because the cleaning lady has only just disappeared from sight behind the doorframe before she reappears, this time in the company of Chloe's older sister—and as soon as Abby has entered the room, the cleaning lady grabs her cart and quietly tiptoes out.

"Hey, sis. How are you?"

"Okay, I guess," Chloe replies, although she actually isn't entirely sure how she feels.

"The mask bothering you?"

"It's a bit tight."

"Yeah, I can imagine."

"Where, um ... where are Mom and Dad?"

"They're okay," Abby hastens to say. "They just need a bit of fixing. Mom's fingers and Dad's ... well, burns and the gunshot wound, you know. He's got a bit of everything. But they *are* okay. I promise."

"I believe you," Chloe replies—and that is the truth. Still, she can feel the tears pressing on. "And what about you? Are you okay?"

"Yeah, I'm fine. The scrape on my back looks pretty awful, but they've put some cream on it that numbs it, so I can barely feel it. The rest are minor things, and the doctors say I'll be okay as long as it doesn't get infected. Aren't you going to ask what I've got behind my back?"

Chloe tilts her head and stares at Abby, who, sure enough, has one hand hidden behind her back. She hadn't even noticed it until now.

"What do you have behind your back?"

"Ta-da!" Abby says, holding out a game box. An old,

worn version of Monopoly. "It's the Disney edition. It's got *Sleeping Beauty* castles instead of hotels. I found it in the common room. I thought we could play a game. We might as well make the best of it if we're spending Christmas Eve in a hospital, right?"

Chloe looks away for a moment. Then she turns her gaze back to her older sister—now blurred by a veil of tears—and nods.

"I'd like that, Abby. I'd like that very much."

*December 25th,
One Year Later*

Adam

"Beth? Are you awake? The girls are up. I can hear them sneaking around out there."

Beth blinks her eyes and stretches under the covers. Then she sits up with a jolt.

"It's Christmas morning," she says. As if *he* needs a reminder.

"It sure is," he replies, after which he takes her left hand and kisses the back of it. It's something he has made a point of doing every single day since she lost two of her fingers. Sure, she says she hardly even thinks about it anymore, but he still notices how that hand tends to find its way into her jacket pocket when they're out. And he definitely doesn't want her thinking it bothers him in the slightest.

He glances over at the window where the sun's first rays are starting to filter through the blinds, casting a pattern of broad, horizontal stripes of light and shadow across the bedroom walls.

"We'd better get up before they open all the presents," Beth whispers, kissing him on the cheek.

Adam nods and sits up on the edge of the bed. From there, he is able to reach the cord for the blinds, which he grabs and pulls.

The frosty morning outside the window is blinding, and it takes a few seconds for his eyes to get used to the light.

The rooftops in the town are bright white. It snowed last night. That's a sight he still has conflicting feelings about. Certainly, a part of him enjoys it, since a blanket of snow is always the icing on the cake on Christmas morning. Another part of him is instantly sent a year back in time.

He shakes off the memory and gets on his feet. Beth is already out of bed. She is standing over by the closet, putting on a woolen cardigan. When she is done, she throws a sweater to him.

Reindeer with Santa hats and flashing noses. The ugliest piece of clothing in his possession. Just as it should be on Christmas Day.

As they sneak out of the bedroom, they hear their daughters' excited outbursts coming from the living room. This makes both him and Beth pick up the pace. They round the corner and enter the living room where the girls are.

Chloe is sitting on the floor in front of the Christmas tree, staring at the mountain of gifts piled up underneath it. Behind her, Abby stands, hands on hips, wide smile on her face. True to tradition, neither of them has bothered to change clothes and are still in their pajamas.

"Good morning, girls. And Merry Christmas."

"Good morning, Dad," Abby replies. "Yeah, and to you too, Mom."

"I know which one I'm going to open first," Chloe says, pointing. "That big yellow one."

"Are you sure you don't want breakfast before we start with the presents?"

That joke is also a Christmas tradition in the Gray family. Whether it's delivered by Beth or Adam varies from year to year, but it always comes.

"You're so hilarious, Mom," Abby says dryly, before sitting down on the floor next to Chloe and giving her a loving nudge with her shoulder. "The yellow one is from me. You can open it if you want."

She doesn't have to say that twice. Chloe's hands fly over to the tree and back again in the blink of an eye.

"It rattles," she says, holding the gift to her ear and shaking it.

"Hey, that's cheating! Just open it."

Chloe rolls her eyes as if to say *you're so boring*. Then she places the gift on her thighs and starts unwrapping it.

Adam knows what's inside the big box, and he has a hard time keeping a straight face as Chloe, with increasing confusion, removes the first, second, third, and fourth layers of cardboard—before getting to the bag of plastic buttons they added to make sure the box would rattle when Chloe shook it.

"Is that ... buttons?" Chloe asks. "What am I supposed to do with those?"

"Try opening the bag," Abby replies.

Chloe—still confused but willing to play along—opens the bag and puts her hand down among the buttons. When she pulls it up again, it's holding two small pieces of paper.

"What is ... no! For real?" Chloe exclaims, staring at her older sister with disbelieving eyes. "You're kidding me!"

"Nope. Two tickets to the concert with Neo-Neon. You and me. Mom and Dad said they'd let us go on our own."

"*If* we drive you there and pick you up afterward," Adam adds.

"Yeah, yeah. They deliver and pick up," Abby repeats, shaking her head. "What do you say? Isn't it cool? A concert with your favorite band—and you get to go with your favorite sister."

"It's the best gift ever," Chloe says, wiping her eyes. "I mean it. Thank you, Abby, I ... I love you."

"You're welcome, sis. I love you too."

Behind the two girls, Adam exchanges a glance with his wife, and she nods because she knows what he's thinking.

We actually did it. We came out on the other side.

All four of them jolt when the shrill, metallic ringing from the doorbell suddenly cuts through the air.

"On Christmas morning?" Adam mutters, squinting his eyes. "That's got to be a mistake."

He looks at Beth to see if she has any idea, but she just shrugs.

"I'll go out and check," he says. "You don't have to wait for me to open the next one ... but keep your filthy paws off my gifts."

"Oh, we will," Beth says, laughing as she winks at Abby and Chloe. "Right, girls?"

"Riiight."

"Gee, how convincing," Adam says, after which he turns around and moves through the house until he reaches the entrance.

It's dark in the narrow hallway, so he instinctively reaches to the wall and lets his fingertips slide along the wooden panels until they find the light switch.

He never turns it on, though, as his focus is stolen by something else. Something that slows the blood flow in his veins and fills it with ice crystals.

It's the frosted glass pane in the front door. There's something on the other side of it.

There's something *hanging* on the other side of it.

Reluctantly, he takes a step forward. Then another. He doesn't want to, but he needs to know for sure.

And he does now, when the contours sharpen, and the unmistakable red color of the Christmas stocking penetrates the frosted glass. *Bleeds* through it.

THE END

Afterword

Dear Reader,

Welcome to the afterword. Whether it took you 25 days to get here or not, I'm pleased that you've arrived—and I hope you enjoyed the journey.

I certainly did, although I must admit it was a strange feeling writing a Christmas story in the middle of summer. Especially since I live on the southern coast of Spain, and my desk has a view of the Mediterranean Sea. Not much 'snowy holiday' about that.

Luckily, I grew up in Denmark, so I still remember what it feels like when the world turns white and the cold numbs your fingers.

Having to imagine snowy mountains in December wasn't the only challenge, though. You see, normally my stories start with an idea for the events, often in the form of a *what if* question. An obvious example would be my novel *DRY*, which started with the question:

What if all the oceans suddenly disappeared?

25 DAYS, on the other hand, began in a different way. It started with my wife and I toying with the idea of me writing a Christmas-themed horror story. She is an avid horror reader, and she really felt there was a demand in the horror community for a Christmas story with a dark edge.

All good and well. The only problem was ... well, me. I didn't want to do it unless there was a solid story idea, and the only thing I really had was a faint image in the back of my mind. A Christmas stocking dripping with blood.

Then one day, while drinking our daily coffee at our usual café, the *what if* question came to me—only this time, it wasn't about the plot but rather the structure of the story.

What if the horror story came in the form of an advent calendar? 25 days, 25 chapters.

Brilliant, right? Well, I thought so, and I soon started plotting the story. However, this turned out to be a bigger task than I had imagined because having the events occur on the given date means that something interesting has to happen each day for 25 consecutive days, and you can't skip more than a few hours ahead at a time.

Oh, and just to make sure it didn't get too easy, I

gave myself the additional challenge of using a rotating point of view, so it alternates clockwise between Adam, Beth, Abby, and Chloe. This locked the viewpoint to a certain character—and sometimes they weren't the center of the action. For instance, when Adam finds the rabbit's foot in the stocking, I had to show it through Abby's eyes. All because of my stupid, self-imposed rule.

As challenging as it was, I had a lot of fun writing this story. Granted, it was different, especially at first, because it was motivated more by a concept than an idea. Gradually, though, the characters and the story began to take center stage, and my initial worry—that it might not end up feeling like one of my stories—faded.

Looking at the finished story now, I'm happy to say that I do feel it turned out well. Furthermore, what started out as a fun idea for the structure actually ended up strengthening the story. At least, that's how I feel—and I hope I'm not the only one.

Well, I think that just about sums it up. All that remains is to say thank you to the wonderful people who helped me get this book across the finish line.

They are *Sarah Jacobsen*, my eternal first reader and co-conspirator in this life, and *Kaare & Karina Bertelsen Dantoft*, my dynamic beta reader duo.

Last—but never least—I owe the usual thanks to you, dear reader. Our time is valuable, and I'm honored

that you decided to spend some of yours reading my
words.

—PER JACOBSEN

Printed in Great Britain
by Amazon

51655286R10202